MEET THE WARM AND WONDERFUL SMITH FAMILY!

Chad, the father, is a hard-working detective on the police force of a small suburban town in the Los Angeles area.

Betty, his wife, is young, lively, smart, and very much concerned with the well-being of her husband and children.

Cindy, the eldest child, bright, sensitive and extremely pretty, finds that the daughter of a detective faces special problems these days.

Bob, the middle son, is an attractive, amiable but firm-minded young man, whether the issue is the length of his hair, or a matter of wider importance.

Brian, the youngest, is sturdy and inventive and, like many another family "baby" has learned to turn some of the disadvantages of his position into advantages.

This thoroughly delightful book is based
on the popular A.B.C. television show
"The Smith Family," starring
Henry Fonda

The Smith Family #1

Meet The Smiths

Norman Daniels

A BERKLEY MEDALLION BOOK
PUBLISHED BY
BERKLEY PUBLISHING CORPORATION

Copyright © 1971, by Berkley Publishing Corporation

All rights reserved

Published by arrangement with American Broadcasting
Company Merchandising, Inc.

SBN 425-02127-0

BERKLEY MEDALLION BOOKS are published by
Berkley Publishing Corporation
200 Madison Avenue
New York, N.Y. 10016

BERKLEY MEDALLION BOOKS ® TM 757,375

Printed in the United States of America

BERKLEY MEDALLION EDITION, JANUARY, 1972

CONTENTS

PERSONAL AFFAIR

Cindy Smith said, "I'd better put Dad's food in the oven, Mom."

"He's sure late tonight," her fifteen-year-old brother, Bob, remarked.

Betty Smith, mother of eighteen-year-old Cindy, Bob, and seven-year-old Brian, had made it a rule not to express any worry when her detective sergeant husband didn't arrive home on time. A policeman's hours, she had learned long ago, were anything but regular, and if Chad didn't phone to say he'd be late, it was because he was unable to do so.

They were on dessert when they heard the familiar sound of the car pulling into the driveway. Betty went to the window and drew back the curtain as Chad got out of the car. She ducked back quickly, because she didn't want him to see her looking out, a betrayal of the fact that she was worried.

"Mom," Brian said, "can I tell him right away, please?"

"About what?" Betty asked.

"My hamster. Dad has got to like him. Honest, Mom, I can't let him go now. He's . . . he's like a brother to me."

"Ohhhhh, brother," Bob groaned. "Now I'm related to a hamster."

Chad limped slightly, a fact that Betty hadn't noticed, and he pulled himself up to present the best possible appearance before his family. It was, he decided after looking down at his coat and trousers, not such a good appearance at that. He walked into the house.

"Hi, gang," he greeted everyone cheerily. "Sorry I'm late. One of those things."

He walked to the closet where he hung up his coat, and placed his gun and handcuffs on the top shelf. Betty arose quickly before he could close the closet door.

"Chad, your coat! It's ripped . . . look at that. A pocket almost clean off, a lapel hanging by threads. And your pants. . . . Chad, you've been in a fight."

"I bet the other guy looks worse," Bob called out.

Betty said, "Cindy, fetch your father's dinner from the oven. Be careful now, the plate will be hot. Chad, are you all right? You're not hurt?"

"Oh, heck no. It wasn't much of a tussle. I've got a sore leg where I was kicked, but that'll be okay by tomorrow."

"There's a definite bruise alongside your jaw," Betty said critically. "It's swollen a little."

"I got clobbered some," Chad admitted as he sat down.

"Did you arrest the other man, Dad?" Brian wanted to know. "Did he have a gun and a knife, and you took them away from him?"

"You read too many comic books," Chad said. "There were three of them, in fact. Three crazy kids."

"What did happen?" Cindy asked, as she placed the plate of hot food before her father.

"It didn't amount to much. I was on my way home, going down Venice Boulevard. There's a big warehouse owned by a man named Porter. Anyway, I saw a small crowd outside the warehouse, so I stopped. Porter explained that there were three men inside, armed and dangerous, and they were searching the warehouse for something. They'd assaulted him and two of his men, and told them if they called the police, they'd blow the place up."

"And you went in after them," Betty said, somewhat patiently, but proudly too.

"Somebody had to, with that bomb threat," Chad said. "You know, there wouldn't have been any trouble if Porter and the others lent me a hand. Porter didn't even want me to go in. Said he'd blame me if the warehouse was blown up. He refused to call for help and ordered his employees not to do so. There were fifteen or twenty people who lived and worked in the area gathered around too, but not one offered to lend me a hand. I asked for volunteers to cover the rear exit, and nobody volunteered. I didn't have a radio in my car so something had to be done quickly. I was afraid to use the phone in the warehouse office, because if those three crazy kids meant it, about the bomb, they just might set it off. So there was only one thing to do. I went after them."

"Boy," Bob said, "I'll bet that was some fight."

"As a matter of fact, it didn't last long," Chad said. "They heard me coming. They didn't know I was a police officer. One of them let me go past him while he hid. The other two baited me into the open and the one behind me jumped on my back. I wrestled him around. That's how my clothes got torn. We rolled on the floor some. One of the other kids kicked at me. I finally got to my feet and, I'm sorry to say, pulled my gun. They didn't make a move after that. I held them right there because I was afraid to herd them out to the street. The warehouse consists of scores of little rooms where things are stored. I hoped somebody would finally call for help."

"And nobody did," Betty said. "I'll just bet they didn't move an inch while you were in there, risking your life to save that man's warehouse."

"No, they didn't send for help. Not until I finally marched my three prisoners out. Then they all tried to phone. They acted as if they'd backed me up all the way. Honestly, I had to laugh at them. They were big heroes."

"Who pays for your suit?" Betty asked. "Oh, Chad, this has happened so many times."

"Well," Chad said, "there are no provisions for replacing a suit, so I'll have to buy it myself."

"It wasn't a month ago you told me you couldn't afford a new suit this year."

Chad grinned slowly at her. "That was when I had two suits. Now I don't have a spare, so I have to get a new one. Makes a difference. Know something? This is one fine dinner. Thanks for keeping it hot."

"At least you get some cooperation around your own house," Cindy said. "I'm ashamed of people who won't help a police officer. Do they expect you to fight all their battles?"

Chad's grin grew wider. "Reminds me of what Mr. Porter said when I asked him to go in with me and show me around the warehouse. He said I was paid to arrest criminals. He wasn't, so I'd better go earn my pay."

Brian had waited, saying nothing, but he could contain himself no longer. His father was no doubt a big hero and he'd arrested three men all by himself, but Brian's problem was of vital importance to him.

"Mom? Now? Can I now?"

"Can you what?" Chad asked, glad the conversation had shifted.

"One of Brian's friends gave him a hamster, and Brian wants permission to keep it," Betty explained.

"It's a great big rat," Cindy exclaimed with a shudder.

"It is not," Brian cried out. "It's no rat! It's a beautiful hamster and I want to make him my friend. Dad, may I keep him?"

"Not in the house," Cindy said. "If that thing roams around, I'll have to keep my door locked."

"Well, you can keep it locked if you want to. No hamster ever hurt nobody," Brian said. "Dad, can I? Huh? Can I?"

"We'll have a look at him after dinner," Chad said.

"Now, Dad. Please? Right now? I got him in a box and I don't think he likes it there."

"Where do you intend to keep him except in a box?" Cindy asked. "Maybe you'll take him to bed with you?"

"I wouldn't mind. I love him. He's beautiful."

"After I finish my dinner," Chad said. "I'd like a second helping if there is any. You know, a little exercise like I just had is good for the appetite."

"Don't joke about it," Betty pleaded. "You might have been badly hurt."

Chad changed the subject to that of hamsters which delighted Brian and made Cindy begin the dishes a bit earlier than usual. Bob went to the kitchen to help her.

Chad let Brian lead him to the garage where, in a large cardboard box, the hamster was backed into a corner. Before him was a mound of food, enough for fifty hamsters. He was nibbling daintily on a bit of lettuce.

"Gosh," Brian exclaimed in a worried voice, "he didn't eat hardly anything."

"If he stuffed himself from that pile of food, you'd never

be able to notice it," Chad said. "He looks fat and healthy to me."

"Can I keep him, Dad? Please?"

"Yes, you may keep him. I'll get busy and make a cage for him. You're not to set him free in the house. I want that understood. You and I, and maybe Bob, aren't afraid of a little animal like this, but women don't like anything that resembles a rodent."

"What's a rodent?"

"A rat."

"He's no rat," Brian shouted. "He's a beautiful hamster."

"Okay. Calm down. He's a hamster and not a rat. Now go fetch me that roll of wire net in the corner. I'll get my tools and some lumber. Won't take long to make a cage."

"A big one, Dad, so he can run around?"

"Within reason, son. Within reason."

The cage was a success. The hamster appreciated it by rolling into a ball and falling asleep. Brian insisted on staying in the garage to watch him. In case he gets sick, he explained. Chad returned to the house.

He had settled down with the evening newspaper, when Betty went to answer the door. She returned with a portly man of about forty, and a small boy holding on to his hand. Chad laid aside his paper and arose quickly.

"Hello, Mr. Porter," he said. "I'd like you to meet my wife. Betty, this is Mr. Porter, the man who owns the warehouse where I had a little trouble this afternoon."

"How do you do, Mrs. Smith," Porter said. "You have a remarkably brave husband."

"I'm aware of that," Betty said, somewhat icily.

"And this is my son," Porter said. "Steve, you may shake hands with the nice lady and with the detective sergeant."

"How do you do," Steve said politely. He turned to Chad. "How do you do, sir."

"Hello, Steve," Chad said. "I've got a son just about your age."

As if he'd called him, Brian came rushing into the house, to stop abruptly and stare quite frankly at this new boy.

"This is Brian," Chad said. "Brian, this is Steve, and his father, Mr. Porter."

"You want to see my hamster?" Brian asked.

"Sure . . . gosh, you mean he's alive?" Steve asked, and an immediate friendship was cemented between the boys. They went racing out of the house.

Porter accepted Chad's invitation and sat down. "I came to apologize," he said. "A man can be so wrong under stress. I was afraid they were going to blow up my warehouse."

"I understand that," Chad said tolerantly.

"People," Betty said crisply, "shouldn't expect a policeman to do everything alone. There are times when he needs help."

"You're so right, Mrs. Smith. That's what I'm apologizing for. I should have helped, but . . . well . . . to be frank about it, I was too scared to go into the warehouse."

"Let's just drop the subject," Chad said, sure that Betty was getting up a fresh head of steam.

"Tell me," Porter asked, "did they confess to you what they were after?"

"No. I didn't question them. I turned them over to the burglary detail. If you wish, I'll call in and see what's happened."

"I'd appreciate it, Sergeant."

Chad went to the phone. Betty relaxed somewhat. "Do you live around here, Mr. Porter?"

"About a mile away. My wife asked me to invite you

and your husband to dinner Sunday. We want to do something to repay him for what he did."

"He expects nothing, Mr. Porter. No police officer does. It's just his job. He gets paid for it."

Porter winced. "Seems to me I remember making a point of that too. That's what I'm trying to make up for. My wife and I would be very pleased if you'd come and bring the family. Steve and your son should get on famously."

"Very well," Betty said, on the theory that maybe Chad should get something for what he'd done.

"Another thing," Porter said. "Your husband's clothes were pretty well ripped in the fight. I want to present him with a new suit."

"Please don't mention that in front of him," Betty said. "He won't like it, I assure you. He'll buy his own suit."

"Of course. I shouldn't have mentioned it."

Chad returned from the telephone. "Those three kids, as I called them, were a little above that category. They were not teenagers and all three were released from prison not two weeks ago. They're on parole, so that means they'll go back. Meanwhile, they've made no statements and they're dickering for bail."

"You don't think they'll come back?" Porter asked anxiously.

"I don't know," Chad said. "Obviously they were after something that's stored in your warehouse. It might be loot from previous robberies. It might be something that another convict they met in prison stored away and asked them to get."

"They could come to me with a release order," Porter said. "That's a simple way to do it."

"Providing they could get a release order. It may be they're after whatever is in one of the storage rooms without the consent of the man who put the stuff there. Or, being professional burglars, they may not believe in paying for something they can steal."

"Don't mention this to my wife," Porter begged. "I'm not a brave man, but she'd go to pieces if she thought those three would come back. They said they would, you know, if I called the police."

"Unless they get bail—and it's quite high—they won't bother you again. Meanwhile we'll try to determine what they were after and what compartment it's stored in."

"Mr. Porter has invited us to dinner on Sunday," Betty said.

"Oh? Good! That's fine," Chad said. "Maybe by then I'll have more definite information about those three, and what they were after."

Porter arose. "Thank you very much, Sergeant. And you, Mrs. Smith. I'll get my son, if you'll show me where he might be."

"In the garage," Chad said. "I'll go with you."

Porter and his son drove away ten minutes later. Brian reluctantly agreed to go to bed. Bob was doing homework, and Cindy was visiting friends half a block down the street.

Chad had finished the paper. "Porter isn't such a bad fellow," he observed. "His son and Brian got along famously."

"Any kid visiting another kid who has a hamster would get along just fine."

"You're still sore," Chad said. "You know, Porter was scared. He's not accustomed to things like that happening around him this afternoon. A man never knows what he'll do under stress."

"Does that also explain why nobody offered to help?" she asked. "You said there were fifteen or twenty people around."

"They don't want to get involved," Chad said. "Mostly

because of personal fear. Of being hurt or being plain bothered by events that may come out of their cooperation. That's why they hang back. Now and then you get an eager beaver who'll pitch in out of sheer bravado. Those kind I don't particularly like because they can blunder into a mess and make it worse."

"People used to be proud to help an officer," Betty reminded him.

"Yes, that's true, but habits and policies change. A cop used to be respected by everyone, rich and poor alike. Now they're called names, until someone needs them. Then they're a paid servant to go in and risk their necks. If they get hurt, that's to be expected. If they make a successful arrest and deal with the situation, what the heck, that's what they're paid for. And you know something, my sweet?"

"Yes," she said. "You wouldn't stop being a cop for anything."

"Got so you can read my mind. Well, I mean it. It's dirty work sometimes, but it has to be done and it's the kind of work I do best. Helping people. Straightening them out, and all the names I'm called roll off me easily."

"All right, Chad," Betty said. "I agree with all my heart. I wouldn't want you to be anything but a police officer. And, we did get a dinner invitation out of it."

"Maybe a couple of new friends too," Chad said. "That's important."

They had their Sunday dinner at the Porters and Betty found Mrs. Porter an enjoyable woman with many interests similar to her own. Brian had brought along his caged hamster and he and Steve disappeared somewhere with it. Cindy discovered that there was another member of the Porter family, a handsome young man just a year or two older than she. Bob, included in the conversation between his father and Mr. Porter, found his opinions and ideas listened to with respect. He enjoyed himself.

"They are nice people," Betty admitted. "I guess you're right. A man sometimes can't rise above fear. If Mr. Porter was scared because he was thinking of his family, I can see why he would be."

"Sure he was thinking about them," Chad said.

"And you were thinking of yours?" she asked with a smile.

"Well, subconsciously, of course. Mainly I was just thinking how the heck I could round up three young hoodlums all by myself, without getting torn apart. And being plenty mad at all those people who wouldn't lift a finger to help me. Or even a telephone. It's over. I like Porter. I'm glad we met."

"Steve's coming over to visit Brian, though I suspect it's more to visit Humbolt."

"Who is Humbolt?" Chad asked. He grinned. "The hamster! What a name! Well, tomorrow I'll see about a new suit. I have to put my best one into use right away. I think perhaps I'll get a green one this time. Just to be different."

"Green?" Betty asked. "You have to be kidding."

"What's the matter with green?"

"Nothing," she said. "Nothing at all. Of course they'll say, 'Here comes the green detective.' You'd be a stand-out for sure."

"Well, you've got something there. It's handy being married to a clever wife. It's even better to be married to a beautiful one."

"Thank you, dear. Dark brown, that's what it ought to be."

"Yes, dear," he said.

She looked up with a smile. "You've been kidding me!"

"If you believe that, maybe I'll get the green suit."

"Brown," she said.

The following week was a regular semester break in grade schools and Brian was home all day. Betty left him playing with Steve and the hamster named Humbolt. Bob was at school and Cindy at college. Chad, on his way to a routine assignment, using a squad car, was jerked to attention when his name came over the radio.

"Calling Sergeant Smith. Chad Smith. Emergency. Check in, Sergent Smith."

Chad pulled to the curb, picked up the phone and identified himself. The dispatcher connected him with someone in the detective bureau. Chad didn't ask who it was.

"Sergeant, we had a phone call from your son five mintues ago. He says something terrible has happened and you're to come home right away."

"Thanks," Chad said. He hung up, switched on the red lights, started the siren and began the eight-mile drive home at the highest speed he dared risk. Betty hadn't put in the call, so perhaps something had happened to her. He was in a cold sweat as ideas for a dozen catastrophes entered his head. He pulled into a safety lane when a car ahead of him refused to pull over to his siren, cut back into the regular lane and kept going.

He did shut off the siren and lights when he drew near his neighborhood, because if anything had involved Betty, he wouldn't want her to think he was so worried he'd come home at top speed.

Everything seemed quiet when he pulled into the driveway. He jumped out of the car and ran to the front door. It was locked. He got out his key, let himself in.

"Betty?" he called loudly. "Betty? Anybody home?"

There was no answer and his fears grew greater. He

hurried through the house. Nothing was disturbed. He paused to reason things out. Bob and Cindy were at school. Betty had said she was going downtown. Only Brian was home. Brian!

Chad went out the back door and walked to the garage. There he found Brian and Steve, kneeling beside the hamster's cage. Brian looked up through tear-filled eyes.

"He's dead. What took you so long? Humbolt is dead."

"He just curled up and died," Steve added. "We didn't do anything to him."

Chad stifled a sigh of relief. He picked up the animal and examined him. "He's alive. I can feel a heartbeat and he's breathing."

"No kidding!" Brian was on his feet. "Dad, you got to take him to the vet. Please . . . to save his life. He's awful sick."

"Sure is," Steve added, to confirm Brian's anxiety.

"All right," Chad said. "We'll take him to the vet. But Brian, you're not to call headquarters for any reason except one involving people. Do you understand? It has to be important."

"Sure, Dad, but it's important to save Humbolt. That's an emergency."

"Sure is," Steve added dutifully.

Chad gave up. He bundled both boys into the car after placing Humbolt on a bed of rags in a small box. Humbolt was breathing with some difficulty, but still breathing.

"Turn on the siren," Brian begged. "This is an ambulance now."

"No siren," Chad said firmly. "Settle back. We'll soon find out what's wrong with your hamster."

He wondered what his captain was going to say when he learned the reason for the emergency dispatch to Sergeant Chad Smith. At least, Chad mused, his son didn't sit by and do nothing. He acted. Maybe not wisely, but he acted. That was a good sign.

The vet examined Humbolt while both boys looked on. He squeezed the animal gently. The hamster burped.

"What have you been feeding him?" he asked Brian.

"All kinds of things. He likes carrots and lettuce and things like that."

"How often do you feed him?"

"Gosh, all the time. Steve and me, we been feeding him all day so he'll be big and strong."

"Overeating," the vet said. "This animal is so stuffed he can hardly move. He'll run it off in no time."

Chad paid ten dollars for this observation, put the hamster and the boys back in the car and headed for home. He looked over his shoulder at the boys, watching the hamster every moment.

"Steve, how long since you checked in with your mom?" he asked.

"Mom's not home, sir."

"Aren't you supposed to call your father now and then, especially when you're away from home all day?"

"Yes sir, but I guess I forgot when Humbolt got sick."

"All right," Chad said. "We'll stop by your dad's warehouse. It's on the way. I wanted to talk to him anyhow."

He pulled up before the warehouse. "You boys stay in the car," he said. "I won't be long."

There was a long platform in front of the warehouse and a large door marked 'Receiving' was open wide. A smaller door led into the office. Chad found Porter busy at his desk. Half a dozen employees looked up when Chad entered, but they went back to work.

"Nice to see you, Chad," Porter said. "Anything I can do for you?"

"Well, first of all, your son is outside in the squad car with my son, and Humbolt the Hamster, who is slightly ill from gorging. I just came from the vet's. I thought you might be worried about Steve."

"The boy takes pretty good care of himself, and when he's with your son, I don't worry about him."

Chad closed his eyes for a moment. "You don't know what you're saying, Mr. Porter. Brian can. . . ."

From somewhere deep in the warehouse a man screamed in terror. Chad, wasting no time, reached for his gun as he raced inside the huge building.

The man who stepped off the freight elevator was in a white uniform and his face was so pale that it matched his uniform.

"Bomb!" he yelled. "There's a bomb up there! It's all set to go off. Clock's ticking away. . . . I saw it. Bomb!"

He evaded Chad's attempt to stop him, rushed out screaming "Bomb! Bomb! Clear out! Bomb!"

"The idiot," Chad said. Then he paused. Porter was backing away from him, terror in his eyes. The office was cleared of all the help. Other men inside the warehouse went rushing out. Chad put his gun away, strolled out to the platform in front. Across the street a score of people were gathered. Among them was Porter.

Chad calmly sat down on the edge of the platform, swinging his legs idly. After a few moments, Porter stepped forward half a dozen paces.

"Aren't you going in and defuse the bomb or something?" he asked.

"Not me," Chad said.

"But Chad. . . . ."

"I've absolutely no desire to get blown to pieces," Chad said.

"You could call the bomb squad. . . ."

"Why should they get blown to pieces? Now don't say it," he added hastily. "We get paid for this, don't we? I want to spend the money I earn, not leave it to my widow."

"But the warehouse . . . it'll be destroyed. There's a million dollars worth of merchandise in there. . . ."

"You call the bomb squad," Chad said. "There are several phones in your office."

"I . . . couldn't go in there . . . no, sir. But you have to, Chad. You must!"

"I don't have to do anything," Chad said. "A cop enforces the law, but he doesn't have to deliberately sacrifice his life. What if the place blows up? Better that than me blow up."

"Well, what are you going to do?"

"Sit here and wait."

"You're a lousy coward," someone from the group shouted.

Chad grinned. "Whoever said that is welcome to go in and defuse the bomb. I won't stop you. You've got the courage to call me a coward. Prove that you're the big hero. Go on in."

There were no takers, but a great deal of grumbling ensued. Not loud, but Chad knew that they were blaming him and believing him cowardly. He swung his legs and looked quite comfortable.

"Chad," Porter said, "I beg of you . . . do something!"

"Make a suggestion," Chad said.

"You have to get the bomb out of there."

"Why me? It's your warehouse. Go get it!"

"You must be out of your head," Porter said angrily. "I don't know anything about bombs."

"What makes you think I do?"

"Some cop!" someone else shouted.

"The door is open," Chad invited them. "Go on in and take care of it."

Porter backed away, expecting momentarily to have the roof of his warehouse blown sky high. "Chad, aren't you going to do anything?"

"Make a suggestion," Chad said again. "One that doesn't involve my getting killed. Because I hold my life just as precious as any of you. A badge doesn't change that."

"You know I'll have to take this up with the Chief of Police and the Board of Police Commissioners," Porter warned.

"They won't go in either," Chad said. "Who wants to get blown up?"

"Call Police Headquarters now," someone shouted from the crowd.

Chad said, "What if I agree to go in? I don't know where the bomb is. Before I can find it, I'll be blown up. What's the sense?"

"The bomb is at the end of aisle three, section two on the third floor," Porter said. "The man who found it told me that a few minutes ago."

"Got a map so I can follow?" Chad asked.

"No . . . no. . . . ."

"Okay. Tell you what. I'll go in if somebody will lead me to where the bomb is placed. Come on now—anybody who works in this warehouse can find the spot. How about you, Porter?"

"I . . . I can't," Porter said. "I just can't do it."

"Hey, Cop," someone yelled, "while you were sitting there with your back turned, two kids just ran into the warehouse."

Chad jumped up. He could see his car from where he

stood. One door was open. Brian and Steve were gone.

Porter said, in fresh horror, "You said Steve was with your son."

"That's right," Chad said. "They both must have rushed into the warehouse."

"Steve. . . !" Porter raced across the street, climbed the steps and ran into the warehouse proper. He showed no trace of fear now. Chad followed him and when he stepped into the elevator, Chad was beside him.

"These crazy kids," Porter said. "Chad, can we save them? Do we have a chance?"

"We might not be able to save ourselves," Chad reminded him.

"I don't care about that. It's Steve . . . he's my son. For heaven's sake, man, don't you worry about your boy?"

"Just as much as you do about Steve. Relax, Mr. Porter. There's nothing to worry about."

"Nothing to worry about? A bomb up there, our kids in the building. . . . ."

"It's no bomb," Chad said. "I was going to tell you about it when the whole thing happened. The boys are not in danger and neither are we."

The elevator stopped at the third floor. Porter stared at Chad. "I thought you were a little crazy out there when you refused to do anything, but now . . . it's your son too. . . ."

"I repeat, it's not a bomb. Those three burglars finally told the truth. In one of your storage rooms there's an old safe, put there by a convict when he knew he was going to prison. It's listed under an assumed name, the rent has been paid for several more years. The safe is full of money, waiting for the con to be released. These three burglars heard about it and were after it. They knew it was a safe and it would have to be blown open because they certainly couldn't carry it out. So they came prepared, with a box that contained explosive, and a timing device that gave them time to get out of the way after they set the clock."

Chad walked down the corridor which Porter designated as the one where the so-called bomb was placed. It had been partially hidden, but had been pulled out into the open and the lid of the box raised and left that way. Chad bent down and lifted the apparatus. A small clock was ticking away.

"When your warehouseman examined the box, he must have set the clock off. I imagine it was run-down, but moving it started the mechanism again. You can see for yourself, nothing is connected. There's no danger."

Porter leaned weakly against the wall. "Why did you do it, Chad? Why did you let us go on thinking it was dangerous?"

"I thought it might not be a bad idea to let you and the others, all of whom balked at helping me before, find out what it's like when a cop refuses to help. You expect everything from us, so long as you don't have to do any sacrificing."

"All right, I admit I was wrong, but there's going to be a lot of trouble about this."

"I don't think so," Chad said. "Everyone out there knows that if a charge is leveled against me, they'll have to admit they were cowardly. Not for the first time, but the second. No one's been hurt. Some egos might be smarting for a while, but not yours, Bill."

"I refused to go in, didn't I?"

"Sure, as long as it was only your building involved. But when your son ran in everything changed. It wasn't just a building in danger, but a human life you cherished. You didn't even stop to think. You just barged in after him."

"I don't feel like a hero," Porter said. "Far from it."

"Nobody feels like a hero," Chad said. "When there's

something to be done upon which lives rest, you just go ahead and do it. That's how cops operate, but not many people stop long enough to think about it and recognize it. Let's find the kids."

Steve and Brian were on the first floor, engaged in cornering the hamster. "He jumped out of the box and out of the car," Brian called to Chad.

"He sure isn't sick any more," Steve added.

"Chase him some more," Chad said. "That's the best medicine for him. Let him run it off. Mr. Porter will take you home, Brian. I've got to go. I'm still on duty."

When Chad emerged, nobody said a word. He gave them a warm smile and continued on to the police car. He backed around, waved to the group as he drove off. Porter was explaining the situation to them.

He would be off duty in another two hours. He'd take time to stop by has favorite clothing store to buy a new suit. It would be brown.

THANK YOU, OFFICER DOLAN

In the Chad Smith house on Primrose Lane, all but one of the family was at the dinner table. Conspicuously absent was Detective Sergeant Chad Smith, the head of the house.

His wife Betty was there, and his daughter Cindy, eighteen, was serving. Son Bob was engaged in talking about the high school football team which he was trying out for and Brian, seven, picked at his food as usual.

"Where," he asked finally, "is Dad? Seems kinda funny he's not here."

"Your father," Betty explained, "is attending a retirement dinner for a friend of his. He'll be home early."

"What's a retirement dinner?" Brian wanted to know.

"It's when somebody quits work for the rest of his life and starts loafing, you dope," Bob said.

"Why?" Brian asked.

His mother answered. "This friend of your father's worked long and well for the firm and in recognition of his services they give him this dinner and, probably a present."

"A watch," Cindy said. "They always give them a watch even if they own six of them. Miriam's grandfather was retired a couple of years ago and he got a watch. He put it on his wrist alongside the one he always wore. There ought to be more originality in these gifts."

"He gets a watch on account of he won't work any more?" Brian asked.

"That's right," his mother said.

"What's he need a watch for if he's not going to work any more?"

"Good question," Bob said. "But I guess even if you're loafing in a hammock you like to know when it's time to eat."

"Does everybody get a dinner and a watch?" Brian persisted. He was at the subject too long and Betty wondered what was on his mind. Sometimes he had good ideas, sometimes they were catastrophic. This subject, being well behind his small-boy comprehension, promised the catastrophic variety.

"No, not everyone. You have to work faithfully and well to earn it."

"Like a reward for being good?" Brian asked.

"That's about the best description I know of," Betty said. "Now eat your dessert. You certainly didn't eat much of your dinner."

"He had a cold hot dog, some cake and cookies, and a glass of milk about four o'clock," Cindy said. "I don't see how he ate anything."

"Snitch," Brian said without animosity. "I was hungry."

Brian said, "Mom, can I talk to you and Dad about something important when he gets home?"

"Why certainly. If it's not past your bedtime."

Brian nodded somberly and drifted away from the table. Bob and Cindy, not being so lucky at their advanced age, got busy clearing the table and getting ready to do the dishes with Betty's help.

Chad arrived home at ten. Brian, protesting vigorously

had been packed off to bed at nine. Bob was studying, Cindy was at a girl friend's down the street.

Chad kissed his wife, hung up his coat and placed his gun and handcuffs on the closet shelf. "Nice party," he said. "There was a long speech that nearly put me to sleep, but the food was okay and Matt's a good friend, so I was glad to go."

"Did he receive a gift?"

"Uh-huh." Chad sat down and relaxed. "A nice watch."

"Don't they ever think of anything else? We had a discussion about it tonight. Brian asked a lot of questions about retirement."

"Do you suppose he's contemplating retirement already?" Chad asked.

"The way he runs around he'll never retire. He wanted to talk to us about something he says is important, but his bedtime interfered."

"I can talk now," Brian said from the doorway. He wore a blue robe over his pajamas. He came forward slowly, half expecting to be sent off to bed again.

"Very well," Betty said. "If you haven't been able to get to sleep because of this talk, we might as well have it now."

"What's on your mind, son?" Chad asked.

"I do traffic duty at school every day."

"We know that," Chad said.

"So does Officer Dolan."

"That I also know," Chad said. "He's assigned to protect the kids in that school . . . let's see now . . . he was there when I attended and that was . . . oh boy, years ago. Everybody who ever went to that school knows Officer Dolan."

"He's going to retire next week."

"Good for him. He earned it," Chad said.

"I remember him too," Betty said. "He was . . . rather portly. . . ."

"Rather," Chad said with a grin.

"What's this got to do with what you want to ask us?" Betty said.

"I think we ought to give Officer Dolan a big dinner and a present."

Chad whistled softly. "Now that's not a bad idea, but it just isn't done in the department, Brian. No retiring police officer is honored that way."

"Officer Dolan ought to be."

"No doubt, but it isn't done."

"Dad, he's been there maybe fifty years. . . ."

"Not quite," Betty said.

"Anyway, all that time there's been no kid ever got hit by a car and he makes all the drivers go slow when they pass the school. Nobody got hurt all the time he's been there. That's being good, ain't it? If he's good, he ought to get a dinner and a present."

"Listen, son," Chad said, "a retirement dinner isn't given to everyone. Many people don't even want it. Dolan's been a good policeman and that's all the present he needs to see him through his retirement."

"Why can't he have a dinner, huh?"

"Because he belongs to a group that's too big to conduct a dinner like that. If it's done for one man, it'll have to be done for all of them, and we have hundreds of men retiring every year. These things take place mostly in small organizations like the one my friend Matt worked in. I'm sorry, Brian, but it's impossible."

"Back to bed," Betty ordered briskly. "Get along now. You have to be at school extra early these days so you can take up your traffic officer duties."

"He oughta have a dinner and a present," Brian insisted.

"I don't care what anybody says."

He trotted off to bed after another warning from his mother. Betty smiled tolerantly. "What will he think of next?"

"He's got an active mind, that's for sure," Chad admitted.

"So Officer Dolan is going to quit," she said. "When I was a little girl, I thought he was indestructible."

"Dolan's an old-fashioned kind of cop. To him it's just a job, except when it comes to protecting kids. I don't think he ever made an arrest that I can recall. Though, yes, there was one. It happened during a parade, years ago. Dolan was marching with a group of cops and a drunk fell off the curb into the street so that Dolan tripped over him. He hauled him in, mostly because ten thousand people saw it happen. For the life of me, I can't think of another pinch he ever made. Though he was mighty good at warning people to behave."

"I think he did his duty well," Betty said. "As Brian mentioned, no child was ever injured at that school by a car while Dolan was there."

"Brian seemed pretty persistent, don't you think?" Chad asked.

"He gets his teeth into something, he doesn't let go easily."

"I'm afraid of what he may do," Chad said. "I could almost see his mind working as we sent him off to bed. Oh well, I like his attitude. Dolan does deserve something but then, so does every cop. The longer I'm on the force, the more I'm certain of this."

In the morning, Brian carefully closed the snaps on his arm band, which designated him as a school traffic officer. He ate breakfast slowly for a change, being so occupied with thinking that he forgot to gulp his food. He kissed his mother absent-mindedly as he departed for school.

When he arrived, Officer Dolan was already there. At the sight of Brian, one of the first students to appear, Dolan squeezed his bulk from behind the wheel of the radio car, made sure his uniform was buttoned, his cap on straight. No one had ever seen a spot on his uniform and his shoes never lacked a shine. He often pointed out this fact to some of the sloppier kids, and many of them changed their ways, to the astonishment of their parents.

Brian gave him a snappy salute which was promptly returned. "Good morning, sir," Brian said.

"Morning, Officer Smith. It looks like it's going to be a nice day."

"Yes sir, it's going to be a nice day."

"Okay, let's go to work. Mind now, when you stand out in the middle of the road, keep your arms out straight, away from your body—like a scarecrow."

"Yes, sir."

"Good. On your way."

Brian shepherded kids across the intersection, receiving an approving nod from Officer Dolan, half a block down the street before the main entrance. Brian took this work with the utmost seriousness.

After all students were inside the building, Brian made his way, not to his class room, but to the principal's office. Mrs. Travers was harrassed and busy, but she stopped long enough to inquire of Brian what he wished.

"I want to fix it so Officer Dolan has a retirement dinner," he said. "And a nice present."

"Officer Dolan? Oh yes. Yes, he is retiring next week, isn't he? Oh, Brian, that's a nice thought you have, but it's out of the question."

"Why?" Brian asked logically.

"Why? Because . . . well, it's not done, that's all. Never done. But I'll tell you what. I'll have the teachers make up a little fund and we'll present him with a box of cigars."

She recalled that Officer Dolan smoked cigars surreptitiously in his radio car and usually reeked of cigar smoke.

"It's got to be more'n that," Brian insisted.

"It can't be. That's all, Brian. Go back to your class now. Thank you for suggesting it."

Brian walked away slowly. He went to class but he might as well not have been there, because his mind wasn't on ordinary subjects as math and reading. Instead, he was actively scheming and, for a seven-year-old, he was expert at it.

At noon he sacrificed his allowance fund to pay for a bus trip downtown. He wound up in the lobby of Police Headquarters, an ornate, huge building alive with people. There were guards at the doors, but they paid no attention to a small boy, so he got in without trouble. There was an information booth in the lobby and he approached it confidently.

"I want to see the Chief of Police," he said.

The sergeant in the booth leaned over the counter for a better look at his small visitor.

"Oh, you do. And what's your problem, my boy?"

"I want to see the Chief of Police."

"You told me that. What for? To see the Chief you have to have a reason."

"I want to talk to him about a policeman."

"I see. What happened? Were you told to go home?"

"No, sir."

"What have you got against policemen then?"

"Nothing, sir. My dad's a cop. Sergeant Chad Smith. He's a detective."

"Oh, that makes a difference. You want to see the Chief about your father?"

"No, sir. About Officer Dolan."

"Now who is he, may I ask?"

"He does traffic duty at my school and he's going to retire next week and I think he ought to have a retirement dinner and a present."

The sergeant in the booth didn't say anything for a long moment. "Son, where'd you ever get grand ideas like that? I've a mind to send you along to see the Chief. But he's a very busy man."

"I won't stay but a minute," Brian promised.

"Why Officer Dolan?"

"Because nobody ever got hurt in forty years he's been doing traffic duty at my school."

"That's a fine record. But you see, son, if I send you to see the Chief, he'll get sore at me. He has so many important things to do. I'm all for what you want. I'm right on your side, but I like it here in this booth and I don't want to go out on a beat, which is likely to happen if I send you upstairs. I'm sorry."

"Who can I see about it? Gosh, I don't see why the Chief should be so busy he can't talk about a dinner and present for Officer Dolan. It's important."

"So it is—to you. What's your father say about it?"

"He says cops don't get a dinner and a present."

"He's right too. You see, I can't violate the rules by letting you see the Chief, but more important, I can't let you do something your father wouldn't approve of. I'm sorry."

"Who is the Chief of Police's boss?" Brian asked.

"Well—the Mayor, I guess you might say."

"Thank you," Brian turned away, sorely disappointed. The sergeant watched his small figure move toward the exit.

"I wonder if I should have said that," the sergeant murmured. "Oh, they'd never let him in the mayor's office. Boy, that kid's got something, but he's up against the rules."

City Hall was even busier than Police Headquarters and Brian was caught up in the rapid movement of people, so that it took him some time to find the mayor's office. He peeked into the reception room several times when the door opened to admit or exit visitors. Brian had a rather good idea he'd never get to see the mayor by merely asking. His experience at Police Headquarters convinced him of that.

There was a determination in him that refused to be squelched. He finally opened the door, slipped inside and immediately sat down beside a man with a briefcase on his lap. He sat so close it looked very much as if they were together. When one of the secretaries saw him, Brian smiled confidently at her and she couldn't resist smiling back. She didn't ask him any questions but accepted him as being with the man beside him.

When this man was finally called, Brian arose with him and trailed right behind him. The man had no knowledge of this. He opened the door to the mayor's office. Brian caught it before it closed and moved in behind him. There was a row of large chairs to one side of the office. Brian quietly occupied part of one of them, waiting patiently for the man with the briefcase to conclude his business. When he did, and went out, Brian slid off the chair and walked briskly up to the mayor's desk.

The mayor looked startled at first. Then he grinned.

Brian liked him at once. "Well," the mayor said, "who are you, and how did you get in here?"

"I just walked in, sir. I got to see you."

"Very well. You're seeing me. What's on your mind?"

"I been to the principal of my school and she said no. I tried to see the Chief of Police, but they wouldn't let me in. So I got to see you."

"It must be important if you tried to talk to those people. What is it, son?"

"Will you help me, sir?"

"Sure, if I can. Someday you'll be a voter."

"It's about Officer Dolan."

"A policeman?"

"Yes, sir. My father's a policeman too. His name is Sergeant Chad Smith. He's a detective."

"And what is the connection, my boy?"

"Officer Dolan is going to retire next week and I think he should have a big retirement dinner and a present."

"Good heavens," the mayor gasped. "What an idea! Who put it up to you? Your father?"

"No, sir. He said it can't be done."

"He's right, son. It can't be done. You see, the department is too big and we can't play favorites."

"Nobody ever got hurt at school where he does traffic duty. Not in a long time. I guess fifty years maybe."

"That'll be on his record. He will retire with dignity and the thanks of the whole city. That's all, son. I'm sorry."

"Don't you think he ought to have a dinner and a present, sir?"

"Yes, of course I do, but I've tried to explain. Talk to your father about it some more."

"You ain't going to help me, sir?"

"I can't. My hands are tied. Good day, son. I'm glad you came by and I wish I could help."

Brian walked slowly out of the office, dragging his feet. The secretaries in the outer office wondered who he was and how he had been admitted to the mayor's private office, but they didn't try to question him. He looked too woebegone and filled with despair.

One of them said, "Well, there goes a tax payer who didn't get what he wanted. Maybe a reduction in the price of lollipops."

Brian came to a stop in the corridor, not sure which way to turn. He felt that it was no use. He'd been defeated everywhere he went and he'd exhausted every possible source of help. His father had disappointed him. His school principal has been sympathetic, but uncooperative. The sergeant in the information booth agreed with him, but could do nothing, and the mayor, the biggest man of all, said he couldn't help either.

In Brian's mind, any or all of them could have helped. They simply didn't want to. Frustration in a small boy doesn't go away quickly and Brian was just as downhearted when he went home, forgetting that he wasn't due there for more than an hour. He'd cut his afternoon classes. He was hungry and he methodically raided the refrigerator, eating without appetite but generously.

Suddenly, he realized what time it was. His mother was apparently next door or shopping, so Brian left without being questioned, and he ran all the way to the school, arriving just in time to supervise the kids crossing the intersection he was assigned to guard.

With all students departed, Brian favored Officer Dolan with the usual salute, this one not very snappy. He walked home slowly, trying to think of a way to accomplish what he was after, and failing to come up with a single new idea.

That evening, Chad Smith came in looking serious. "Where's Brian?" he asked Betty. "That kid. . . !"

"What's he done now?" Betty asked. "He seemed all right to me when he came home from school."

"I don't know where he came home from, but it wasn't school," Chad said. "He's been doing the town looking for help in promoting a retirement party for Dolan."

"Oh no. Chad, what did he do?"

"He talked to his principal, he skipped school, he went to Headquarters and tried to see the Chief. Then he went to the mayor's office. . . ."

"The mayor?"

"That's right. Our son doesn't do things by halves. Nobody knows how he slipped in, but he did. The mayor couldn't help him. Heaven knows where he went after that. I got a call from the sergeant in the information booth at Headquarters and from one of the mayor's secretaries. They were nice about it, but they said Brian must be made to understand that an ordinary cop just doesn't rate a dinner and a present, as Brian calls it."

Brian walked reluctantly into the room sensing the storm that was about to burst over him. Chad took a look at Brian's woebegone expression and the mild anger he'd felt evaporated.

"Brian, I know what you did today. That was wrong."

"Yes, sir."

"I told you getting up a dinner for Officer Dolan was impossible. You should have listened to me and not bothered all those very important people."

"Officer Dolan is important too, sir."

"I know that. I don't deny it, but . . . but . . . oh, hang it! I agree with you and I feel the way you do about it. Still, we can't fight regulations and you might as well learn that now."

"You could have gotten your father into a great deal of trouble," Betty said.

"If you keep on with this, you will get me in a jam," Chad said. He glanced up at Betty. "Imagine what would have happened if there'd been a reporter in the mayor's office? With politics the way they are in this city?"

"I shudder to think," Betty said.

"Well, it's all over now," Chad said. "I'm not going to punish you in any way, Brian, because I sympathize with what you were trying to do. It was a great idea. Impossible, but great. Now, how about dinner? I'm starved."

Brian went to bed that night without the slightest protest. He was exhausted, but he didn't seem as disappointed as he had earlier in the evening.

"I suppose he accepted it," Chad said. "Sometimes life gets a big complicated at his age."

"He'll get over it," Betty said. "But don't let anybody think I'm not proud of that boy. It was a marvelous idea. No adult would ever have thought of it."

"Guess not," Chad agreed. "The mayor wasn't sore about it, but he did think Brian shouldn't be permitted to run around loose like that. Which is a point I'll have to discuss with Brian."

"It was in a good cause. I wouldn't say a word."

"All right, I won't. It was a good cause. We've got an enterprising boy there. A little soft hearted maybe, but that's not bad."

The rest of the evening was quiet. Chad thought it was too quiet, like the portent of something about to happen.

"I get this feeling," he told Betty. "Like the roof is going to fall in. The kids are too quiet."

"Bob's studying. So is Cindy. She has an exam in the

morning. Brian is dead to the world. I looked in on him a little while ago. Want me to whoop it up by turning on TV?"

"I guess not," Chad said. "How about a game of cribbage?"

"Crib? I haven't played that in so long. . . ."

"Neither have I. I guess we've both forgotten how. It's this darned feeling. . . ."

It finally passed. They checked the family at eleven and went to bed. Chad slept well, but Betty didn't. Chad's worry had been transferred to her by some mysterious influence. She too had a weird feeling that something was going to happen.

The newspaper office was so huge and busy that it frightened Brian more than he'd been by Police Headquarters or City Hall. He wandered about without attracting any attention. He entered the newsroom, threaded his way between desks, grinning amiably when hailed by some of the busy people at the desks. At the far end of the room he saw enclosed offices. There were names and titles lettered on the doors, but Brian didn't understand them.

He stopped at the desk of a gray-haired man who looked as if he might be cooperative. "Please, sir," Brian said, "who is the most important guy here, sir?"

The rewrite man rubbed his chin. "Well now, I guess all of us are important, son. I also guess a few are more important than the rest of us, but if you want to know who yells the loudest, that would be Mr. Allenby in the middle office."

"Yes, sir. Thank you, sir," Brian said.

"What do you want with the most important man, son?"

"I got a most important something to ask him, sir. Thank you very much."

Brian, seated on a high stool brought in from the composing room, told his story to the City Editor. He was listened to politely and allowed to relate the whole thing before any questions were asked.

"So you went to see the mayor and he turned you down," the editor reflected.

"Yes, sir. But he was awful sorry he had to."

"Yes, I imagine he was. Did he know you were coming here?"

"No, sir. Nobody did."

"How'd you happen to think of asking a newspaper for help?"

"My dad said if the reporters heard of it, something might happen."

"He's a smart man. Now, Officer Dolan has done traffic duty at one school for forty years or so. We can confirm that easily. During all those years nobody ever got hurt crossing the street. Now that's a record, to be sure. A fine one."

"Yes, sir. That's why I think he should have a dinner and a present."

"Are you willing to risk getting your bottom tanned to go through with this, Brian?"

"Yes, sir. Only my dad won't tan me, sir. He says he agrees with me, but he can't do anything."

"True. Very true. We won't involve him. Now go on home. Don't say anything about your visit here. Your father is going to be surprised. Oh yes, one more thing. Can we take your picture?"

"Sure," Brian said. "Mom would make me put on my good suit if I was home, but I guess I look okay."

"You look fine. Beautiful. I'll send for a photographer. Come to think of it, maybe I'll be in the picture too. We'll stand up like men and be shaking hands. How about that?"

"Yes," Brian said. "How about that?"

It was the following morning when Brian was awakened by a loud shout from the front of the house. It was his father, and Brian shuddered. This was the time of morning when Chad went out to pick up the morning newspaper, and Brian had an idea of what was in it. He pulled the covers over his head.

The door of his bedroom opened noisily. Brian peeked out from the covers. His father stood looking down at him.

"Okay," Chad said. "Brush your teeth, wash your face and comb your hair and then come downstairs. Pronto, understand? No stalling."

"Yes, sir," Brian said. He jumped out of bed and raced to the bathroom. Chad was reading the newspaper article for the fifth time when Brian walked in, properly scrubbed and slicked.

"Take a look at this," Chad said. "It's all about you and Officer Dolan. It's the article featured on the front page under the title of 'THANK YOU, OFFICER DOLAN'. You can't miss it. Your picture is there too."

Brian looked at the article. It was extensive, with more pictures, especially one of Officer Dolan trying mightily to pull in his belly.

"Is this all they're going to do?" Brian asked in an offended voice. "Just say thank you? Honest, Dad, I thought they were going to give him a dinner and a present."

"They are, if you read the whole thing."

"Isn't it wonderful?" Betty asked.

"It will be wonderful, what's going to happen to me," Chad said. "Brian, I asked you not to go on with this. You are supposed to pay attention to your father."

"Yes, sir, I always do. Except this time."

"Do you think they'll really have a party for Dolan?" Betty asked.

"Will they? According to this article and the conversation I already had with the editor, there will be so many people present it's going to be held in the Palladium. Imagine that? The Palladium! They can get thousands in there."

"But on such short notice. . . . ." Betty said.

"This editor got on the phone and had about fifty reporters doing the same thing. They got old records from the school and they called everybody they could reach who'd ever crossed the street under Dolan's protection. This is going to be a retirement party to beat all of them. I'm beginning to wonder if my retirement is going to happen a bit sooner than I expected."

"No, I don't think so," Betty said. "Of course, Brian's the big hero. I'm only his mother. I'll wear my lavender dress. Bob and Cindy will have to be there too, of course."

"Of course," Chad said. "Don't pay any attention to the ribbing I'm going to get from every cop I meet."

"It will be all good-natured. It's wonderful, Chad. It's fantastic."

Chad nodded, glancing at his subdued son. "And all from that little package of TNT. All right, son, you're forgiven, with the understanding that if you get any more brilliant ideas and I say you can't go through with them—you can't."

"Within reason," Betty added diplomatically.

"Yes . . . indeed," Chad gave up.

That night Chad came home early. There would be no dinner at home. That would come later, when Officer Dolan was being honored. Bob and Cindy, excited and happy, were dressing. Betty was trying to decide what costume jewelry she'd wear. Chad sat wearily in one of the living room chairs. Brian was somewhere, likely keeping out of his way.

Betty came down to model her dress. "Beautiful," Chad said. "Not half as beautiful as you, but very, very nice."

She bent down and kissed him. "I can tell you've had a busy day, darling."

"Yes—busy. All day I've been answering the telephone, and in between that, shaking hands with people who congratulated me. You'd think I'd maneuvered the whole doggone thing."

"Was there any trouble? I mean . . . with the Chief or the Inspectors?"

"Not so far, but I don't like the way they're keeping quiet. You know, this is plain blackmail engineered by our son. Now where did he ever get the wonderful idea of going to the newspapers?"

"You gave it to him, dear."

"I did?"

"When you were bawling him out. Later you said something about how lucky it was the newspapers hadn't heard of it."

Chad nodded. "You know, it was a pretty good idea at that. Well, I'd better get dressed. See that Brian wears his best. He's the star of this show and that's no exaggeration."

Chad was having trouble with his necktie when the doorbell rang. Everyone else was busy so he ran downstairs. Betty came down too, before he opened the door.

Chad looked back at her. "Well, it's the Chief Inspector, no less. In full uniform. This is either good or it's very, very bad."

"Oh, Chad, do you think it means trouble?"

"One way to find out," he said, and opened the door. "Good evening, Inspector. I want you to meet my wife."

The white-haired official touched the peak of his cap to Betty and offered his hand to Chad.

"It's going to be a big evening, Sergeant. The Chief ordered me to fetch your son. He'll be seated between the Chief and the Mayor tonight. Officer Dolan is so stunned by it all he's not saying much, and I think his speech of gratitude is going to be a stumbled mess. It doesn't matter. We all know what he accomplished in his life as a cop. Not one student hurt in forty-one years under his protection."

"Yes, sir, it's quite a record," Chad agreed.

"It's also political dynamite. You know how many people graduated from that school in forty-one years? And every one of them votes. Thousands . . . thousands of votes. . . . ."

"It's simply grand," Betty said. "I hope they're not giving Officer Dolan a watch."

"I can't say for the others," the Inspector told her. "We've taken up a collection . . ." he glanced at Chad, "Sergeant, you owe me two bucks. Anyway, we got him a two-week vacation in Hawaii. There'll probably be a truckload of other presents."

"And all from one small boy's imagination," Betty said proudly. "My son's imagination."

"Where is he?" the Chief Inspector asked. "It's getting on, and there are to be a lot of pictures. . . . ."

Brian ran down the stairs. He wore his best suit, everything about him was neat.

The Inspector offered his hand. "Good evening, Mr. Smith. Brian Smith. I'm Inspector Martin come to be your

escort to the retirement dinner in honor of Officer Dolan.
You will be the second in importance to the guest of honor,
him being Dolan of course."

"Thank you, sir," Brian said. "I'm ready. I guess. I . . .
wait a minute!"

He whirled and flew up the stairs. In half a minute he
was coming down them again. He was trying to snap on his
traffic officer's armband. His father gave him a hand at it.

Brian looked up at his father and mother and grinned.

"I almost forgot my uniform," he said.

UPTOWN MAN

Brian Smith, seven, had engaged himself in the art of packing a suitcase, shortly after noon. It was now dinner time and he'd succeeded in stowing about one fifth of the things he believed necessary to the vacation plans of a healthy, energetic boy. Heaped on the floor was a bow and an assortment of arrows. The arrows fit easily, but the bow was oversize by two feet. A stack of comic books a foot high were essential, but he decided he could tie them into a neat bundle. A pair of sneakers, with a hole in the toe of one, were a decided must, so they had never been removed from the suitcase for other items to be squeezed in.

He heard the car pull into the driveway. That meant his father was home. Brian went racing out of the room and was at the door when Chad Smith entered.

Chad scooped him up. Brian pretended he didn't like this. He claimed only little kids were greeted that way though he did admit that shaking hands with his father wasn't exactly the right way either.

"Dad," he said, "can I have another suitcase? Maybe I can borrow Bunkie Carter's old one. I haven't enough room. . . ."

47

"Hold on now," Chad warned. "Where is everybody else?"

Betty emerged from the kitchen, wiping her forehead with the edge of the apron she wore. "Will I ever be glad to get away from the kitchen for a while. Hello, dear. Everything go all right today?"

Chad Smith kissed his wife lovingly. After twenty-one years he didn't know any other way. He went to the closet, removed his coat and hung it up. Then he drew his gun from its holster and placed it on the shelf, adding handcuffs to lie beside it.

Chad Smith was a detective sergeant on the Los Angeles Police Department, but when he walked into this house he stopped being a policeman and became a devoted father and husband. Because his eighteen-year-old daughter Cindy was not home yet and his fifteen-year-old son Bob was busy in the yard, Sergeant Chad Smith began setting the table for dinner, enlisting the aid of Brian when something unbreakable was required.

"I know that sometimes I come back from a vacation more tired than when I left," Betty said, "but how I do enjoy those two weeks. And in two more days we'll be locking up. We'll be leaving the grass to grow and the dust to fall and no dishes in the sink. I think I'm getting a little balmy just contemplating it."

Bob came in, waved a greeting, washed up in the kitchen and was ready to sit down when Cindy burst into the hallway.

"I'm sorry I'm late," she apologized. "I hope nobody's mad at me."

Chad wondered who on earth could be angry at this attractive, wholesome looking girl.

"Of course not," Chad said. "Everybody to the table. I've got an announcement to make."

"Oh boy," Brian said, "maybe we're going to stay three weeks."

"The fact is," Cindy announced, "I'm late because I was held up at the dress shop. I bought the proper clothes for our vacation and I love them."

"Hot pants," Bob said. "I'll bet you got six changes of hot pants."

"Well, what if I have?" Cindy asked impatiently. "They're in."

"They also look nice on you," Chad added.

"Thank you, Daddy. I also bought a dinner dress." She looked around the table. "I presume we will dine at some nice place now and then."

"We will," Betty promised. "Those times will be the highlights of my vacation."

Chad rapped the side of his dish with a knife. "At the start of this meal I told you I had an announcement to make. We were to leave on our annual vacation Saturday—two days from now. We're not going."

"Chad!" Betty cried out in alarm and anguish.

"Dad, you promised. . . . ." Cindy said.

"Hey, what goes on?" Bob asked. "I thought this was for sure."

"I don't go on vacation, I don't go back to school," Brian declared flatly.

"The trip is postponed until a week from Saturday," Chad said.

"But your regular vacation begins Saturday this week," Betty protested, mollified by the fact the vacation was not cancelled but only delayed.

"I arranged to have it begin a week from Saturday," Chad said.

"Well, that's okay with me," Cindy said. "They weren't sure at the dress shop everything could be ready. Now they have plenty of time and I can have more work done on the dinner dress . . . I may even change my mind about it. Honestly, I believe I will. I chose it because it fit me best and needed the least work. . . . ."

"What's a week?" Bob said resignedly.

"I'm kinda glad," Brian said. "I don't think I'd have been ready in time."

"And I," Betty said, "would like to know what this is all about."

"My pleasure to inform you," Chad said. "We intended to have two weeks camping out. Fine—we've done that before and had a lot of fun. But this time there'll be no camping out. We're going to live in the lap of luxury. Everything the very best. And we'll be gone three weeks, not just two. I fixed that."

"Three weeks?" Betty said in amazement.

"In the lap of luxury," Cindy sighed.

"Boy . . . I hope the fishing's good," Bob added.

"Where we going, Dad?" Brian asked, the only practical thinker in the family.

"I'm not going to tell you. It'll be a surprise, and half the fun is being surprised. The other half is surprising people. So we'll all have fun. No questions. I won't even give you a hint except to say this. Cindy, buy two dinner gowns, and your mother is to buy a pair of them as well. Bob, get yourself a new suit. Or a sports outfit if you'd rather that. Now let's eat and forget the whole thing until one week from next Saturday. We're going to live like millionaires."

Later, when Cindy and Betty were doing dishes, Cindy worked at slow speed, her mind too filled with this change of plans.

"Mom, what do you think he meant—we'll live like millionaires?"

"I'm sure I don't know, and I also am sure that it won't

do me one iota of good to ask him for any details. When he wants to be your father is the most closed-mouth person I've ever known. He wants to surprise us, so let's let him. It'll be more fun that way." She paused a moment. "Two dinner gowns for both of us. New clothes for Bob. Something is happening. It must be good. It can't help but be good."

"Of course it is, Mom. But I wish he'd give us a hint."

"He won't. Get busy now. We can't be all night here. I want to check a few fashion magazines. Two dinner gowns! I'm going to be extravagant . . . that is, within reason. And you, too. We're not rich by any means."

"But we're going to live like millionaires," Cindy said, still mystified.

Bob knocked on Cindy's door shortly after nine. He came in wearing a bathrobe and carrying a newspaper. Cindy, just finishing her homework, closed the last book and waited for Bob to tell her why this late visit.

He spread the newspaper on the desk before her. "Did you see this? There's a big story on the police commissioner in New York talking about crooked cops and how he's cleaning them out. The mayor of a big eastern city is going to prison for taking graft or something. Of course I know all cops aren't perfect but . . . so much of it going on, seems like."

"I read the article, yes," Cindy said. "I don't think we have to worry. All you ever hear about is the handful who probably never were good cops to begin with. The thousands who are don't get in the newspapers."

"Yeah, I know, but so much of it going on. That's what the article says. And look at this picture. Barry Barlow's case thrown out of court for lack of evidence. Did you read about him? He's been arrested for almost everything in the book except murder and dope."

"He certainly doesn't look like a crook," Cindy conceded as she examined the picture. "He's really handsome."

"He must be filthy rich. A millionaire, I should think. But I wouldn't change place with him for his and another million dollars."

"Neither would I," Cindy said. "What are you getting at, Bob? You didn't bother me just to show these articles and talk about them."

"I guess not. I think I'm losing my cool completely anyhow, for even thinking. . . ."

"Thinking what? Go on, tell me. I might be able to help you."

"Dad postponing the vacation and saying he'd take another week and we'd live like millionaires."

"Bob Smith, are you insinuating. . . ?"

"No—I'm not. But it makes a guy think. If we can live like millionaires a week from Saturday, why can't we live like millionaires this Saturday? Does one week make all that difference? You think Dad will get a million bucks in one week?"

"I'm ashamed of you," Cindy said, "for even thinking such a thing. Dad was only using a phrase. He didn't mean he'd have a million. If you believe he'd sell out, you're plain crazy."

Bob folded the newspaper and chucked it into Cindy's basket. "I know I am. I was just thinking, and worrying a little so I came to see what my big sister thought. Maybe I am a little goofy, but you don't have to tell me I am. Heck, I know it."

"Go to bed," Cindy said. "With that kind of an imagination you ought to dream well. Dad on the take? It's . . . it's . . . preposterous, that's all."

"Yeah. I ought to have my brains washed out with

soap," Bob confessed. "Good night."

But after he left, Cindy removed the newspaper from the waste basket and read the lengthy story again, while her pretty face grew more and more clouded until she finally brushed the whole thing out of her mind by returning the newspaper to the basket, this time crumpled into a ball.

Saturday, when they were supposed to have begun their vacations, no one seemed to mind that there was a delay. Bob tended his yard chores, Cindy waited impatiently for her gowns to be delivered and that afternoon she and her mother went downtown to pick out Betty's new gowns. Brian had given up trying to pack, postponing that until Wednesday, and he was off playing with some of the neighborhood boys.

Betty and Cindy were on their way to the bus stop after completing their shopping. While they waited for a traffic light to change, a car pulled up. Cindy stifled a gasp by raising her hand to her mouth. She looked anxiously at her mother, but Betty was occupied with a store window behind them. The car pulled away and the crisis was over, but it left Cindy shaken to a point where she could barely carry on an intelligent conversation during their way back.

In the house she went directly to her room and took from a drawer the crumpled newspaper she'd thrown in the waste basket but then recovered and put away. She flattened it out and studied the picture of Barry Barlow, the criminal who had been released for lack of evidence. She'd had a guilty conscience for even saving the article, but that was gone now.

She tore it out of the paper and slipped it into the pocket of her jeans after she'd changed to comfortable clothes. Bob was still at work in the yard so Cindy drifted outside, arousing no suspicion.

"Bob," she said, "I have to talk to you."

"Okay, so talk," Bob answered. He was pruning the hedge, trying to level off a strange hump in the middle of it. He glanced at her. "Hey, what's the matter? You look awful."

"That's how I feel," she said. "Remember the picture of that eastern crook we saw in the paper the other night?" She unfolded the torn paper. "I mean this one."

"Yeah, I remember. We were kind of crazy thinking Dad might be on the take."

"Bob, I saw Dad this afternoon, driving our car, and he had one passenger. This man Barlow. This . . . this . . . crook!"

Bob missed one protruding branch entirely as he swung around to face her. "You sure about that? Maybe it was somebody who looked like him."

"Maybe it was, but it sure looked like the man in the picture. Dad didn't see me and Mom didn't see Dad. I don't know what to do."

"Well, gosh, I don't either. Just because you thought you saw Dad with some guy who looks like Barlow . . . you can't just walk up to Dad and ask him if it's true."

"I know that, silly. We have to find out if it was Barlow."

"Okay, so we find it was. Then what?"

"You're no help," she said. "I might have known a fifteen-year-old boy. . . . ."

"All I did was ask a question. If Dad and this guy have been together, where do we go from there? I don't know the answer. You're in college. With all that education you ought to have some idea."

"Well, I haven't. Besides, I'm not that sure. But it scared me, Bob. It scared me half to death. Dad talking about living like a millionaire and then seeing him with a man I know is not honest."

"Maybe he was arresting him, taking him in," Bob had a bright idea.

"They were laughing and talking like old friends. It was no arrest. I'm sure of that."

"If you think I'm going to ask Dad if he knows this crook and if he's a crooked cop, you're crazy."

"I never suggested such a thing. All I wish is we had some way to make sure this is the same man. Then we'd have a right to ask Dad about it. I think."

"Then let's wait until we are sure. Or forget it!"

Yet Bob was as worried as Cindy. Their enthusiasm for the upcoming vacation was severely dampened. They didn't talk about it, and Cindy had a hard time exclaiming over her gowns, and those her mother had selected.

Sunday had been an especially trying day, for Chad was off duty and spent his time puttering around the house, getting things ready to lock it up for three weeks. Bob stayed out of his way as much as possible, not trusting himself not to blurt out a question that might be wholly uncalled for.

Shortly after the dishes were done, Cindy answered the phone. "For you, Dad," she called to him. "Some man. He didn't say who."

Chad took the proffered phone. "Yes," he said. "Oh—hi. You mean tonight? Yes, I understand that, but . . . well, if it's necessary." He gave a curt laugh. "I'd better be there, eh? Okay, I will. Manny's place in an hour. See you then."

He hung up and sat down in his usual chair. "Got to go out for an hour or two," he told Betty.

"Business?" she asked.

"Not exactly. Friend of mine . . . well, I'd better get started. Have to drive all the way downtown. I'd better change into something presentable too."

He hurried upstairs. Cindy signaled Bob and he met her in the kitchen a moment later. "That was him," she said. "His voice was so sly and smooth. And Dad never said who he was or why he had to meet him. I'm sure it's this man, Bob. We've got to find out."

"What'll we do, ask Dad if we can go along with him?"

"No, silly. But invent an excuse to leave the house right away. I'll give you a few minutes and then I'll say I'm going to see Sally Rivers. I'll meet you at the bus stop. There's an express bus all the way downtown in a few minutes. We might even get there before Dad does."

"Get where? This sounds like a fool stunt to me."

"Dad said he'd meet this man at Manny's. That's a fashionable cafe downtown. I know where it is. If we could get a better look at this man it would help, and I think we owe it to ourselves—and to Dad—to make sure."

"The bus stop," Bob said. "I'll start right away."

The early Sunday evening bus made remarkably good time with few stops, and within half an hour Bob and Cindy got off to walk a block and a half across town to Manny's. It was fashionable, as Cindy had described it. There was valet parking and a few cars were already in the space beside the building. A glance told them their father's car was not there. They checked the street for a sign of it. Apparently they'd beaten him to the rendezvous.

Cindy said, "You stay here and watch for Dad. Don't let him see you. I'm going in. I'm eighteen and nobody will pay any attention to me. If they do, I'll say I'm meeting someone. I'll be as quick as I can."

Bob nodded. He was already as excited about this as he was worried. His worry increased when he saw his father swing the family car into the drive and turn it over to one of the boys for parking. Chad walked into the place and Bob held his breath. He might have met Cindy head on and that would call for some explanations Cindy wouldn't be able to provide.

But after a few minutes she slipped out of the place and joined him. "That was close," she said. "I just happened to see Dad when he came in and I was able to hide."

"Okay, okay. But what about the guy? Is he in there?"

"Yes. I . . . heard Dad ask for Mr. Barlow's table and a headwaiter brought him right to the table and they shook hands like old friends. Dad knows him all right."

"Gosh, this is worse than I thought. What'll we do now?"

"I don't know. I wish we could ask Mom's advice, but I wouldn't tell her about this for the world. And don't you dare," she added sternly.

"Me tell Mom? How could I? There's no mistake? I mean it was light enough in there so you saw the guy good."

"I saw him. There's no question, and if there ever was, Dad took care of that by asking for the man by name. He was meeting Barry Barlow and it's even openly published that he's a crook."

"Let's go home," Bob said. "We'd better be there when Dad gets back or he'll start asking us questions."

They were silent during the bus ride until they were passing through Beverly Hills. Cindy suddenly brought her hand up to cover her eyes, as if she was afraid she might burst into tears.

"What are we going to do, Bob? We can't just accept this. If Dad has been taking money from this man, he's doing it for us. How can we stop him? How can we convince him we don't need any more than we've been having. I never complained—not very much, anyhow."

"I asked for a lot of things I never got," Bob admitted. "I guess Dad couldn't afford it—then."

"Well, it's hard to take. I don't know how I can face him, every morning and every night over the table. Listening to him and Mom making plans for the vacation."

"He's not making any plans," Bob declared dismally. "Because he has to keep everything secret. We'll probably wind up on some yacht headed for Europe or someplace."

"Certainly it's not a camping trip, or he wouldn't have us buy new clothes. Really, Bob, I'm about beat thinking of this."

"Yeah, it's rough. I'm glad Mom doesn't know."

"She'll have to. It will break. It's bound to. If it does, I'm going to stick up for Dad, I don't care what he's done. We know why. He's doing it for us. Oh, darn it. Everything's spoiled. How can we go on vacation knowing it's being paid for by some . . . some crook?"

"We can't back out without explaining, and how do we explain?" Bob said. "So I'm going along with it as if nothing is wrong. That's all we can do."

They managed to slip into the house and reach their rooms without seeing their mother. They heard their father drive the car into the garage about an hour and a half after they got home. They heard his cheerful voice talking to their mother.

How could he be so happy about it? Cindy asked herself that a dozen times. And how could she be happy on a vacation financed in such a manner? She was half tempted to talk to her father privately and reveal all she knew and beg him not to go through with this madness. Or if he had, to give the money back.

It wasn't until Friday that Chad noticed any difference in his family. Brian, of course, was the exception, and Betty seemed well occupied with getting ready for the trip, but Bob and Cindy were too quiet, too somber. At the table they rarely spoke unless they were asked questions.

"Have you noticed the difference in Bob and Cindy?" Chad asked that evening, when he and Betty were alone in the living room.

"Well, come to think of it, yes. They do seem to be acting strangely. By this time—so close to the start of their vacation—they're usually so filled with planning they can't shut up. I don't understand it. They didn't seem to mind the postponement, so that can't be it."

Betty looked at him slyly. "Speaking of the postponement, just what was it all about, Chad?"

"Oh no," he gave her one of his slow smiles. "I said it was going to be a surprise and that's what it will be." His smile faded. "Funny thing, I expected the kids would pester me about it, but they never said a word."

"Brian has talked about it enough. He wants to take along everything he owns. How did you manage to wangle three weeks?"

"I had some time coming. Overtime . . . more than a week. Anyway, it's easy to arrange things when you have people with influence backing you."

"Oh? Do you know someone influential enough to get you an extra week's vacation? I'd like to know the gentleman."

"Tell you about it after the vacation starts. I'm not going to spoil the surprise."

"But Chad, I need more information so I can plan. . . ."

"No," he said good naturedly.

"Oh, all right. Cindy's been asking a few questions, sort of feeling me out to see if you'd confided in me. I can tell her you haven't."

"You do that. They'll get no information from me either."

Chad was too preoccupied that night with his vacation planning to notice that neither Bob nor Cindy came down to say good night as they invariably did.

He came home early on Friday, surprising his family. They were all gathered in the living room. Humming to himself, Chad opened the closet door, hung up his coat, removed his gun from its holster and regarded it for a moment.

"Tonight," he said, "this gets locked up in my strong box until we get back. Believe me, I won't miss lugging it around. And the same goes for the cuffs."

He went upstairs to put the gun and cuffs away. Betty granted Brian's request to be excused until dinner time and he scampered off to his room to try to complete his packing.

Betty said, "Bob, Cindy, what's come over you? Neither of you even greeted your dad, let alone show any pleasure at his coming home."

"We've decided something," Cindy said. "Dad has to be here when we tell what it is."

"My, you sound as if it's of vital importance," Betty said. "And I might add, you two have been uncommonly quiet these last three or four days. Is anything wrong in school?"

"Oh no," Bob said. "Nothing, Mom. I'm doing okay."

"So am I," Cindy said. "This has nothing to do with school. But it is important. We don't expect you to understand, but we mean it. Honestly we do."

"I can hardly wait," Betty said. "It must be important."

Chad returned to the living room and regarded his wife and two of his children. "You all look as if you'd seen a sad movie or something. What gives with all this gloom? You ought to be roaring around getting ready to leave in the morning."

"We've decided we don't want a vacation this year," Cindy said.

Chad sat down heavily. "What's the meaning of that?"

"Just what Cindy said," Bob told him. "We don't want a vacation this year."

"And why not? Or shouldn't I ask?"

"Dad, we don't think the family can afford it. Bob and I have talked it over. We don't want to live like millionaires. I'm going to send back my dinner gowns for refund. We'll just stay home like sensible people and save the money we'd spend on a trip."

"You know what this is all about?" Chad asked his wife.

"I've no more idea than you," Betty replied. "I know something has been brewing, but this is not what I expected."

"It's insurrection," Chad said. "I'm offering you three weeks of loafing, fun, good food, entertainment, fine places to visit and dine. We can afford it. If we couldn't, I'd never have made such plans, but this year, more than any, we can make it with no sweat financially. We've had a good year. I had a raise, we've had no major expenses, even the dental bills have been kept down. So—it's a better vacation than usual this year. Now stop grumbling and playing martyrs. We leave in the morning."

"I'm sorry, Dad," Cindy said. "Our minds are made up."

"Well, so is mine," Chad said, half in anger. "This vacation is meant for you kids as well as your mother and me. We all need to get away for a while and this is our chance. Now you want to muff it without giving any reason. I think I'm entitled to one and I'm sure your mother is too."

Bob and Cindy exchanged glances. They'd agreed that if it came to this, they'd have to tell.

"Well?" Chad asked.

"Barry Barlow," Cindy said. "I'm not going to say more than that, because you'll understand and nobody else will be hurt."

"Now just a moment," Betty broke in. "I'm not going to be left out of this. Who is Barry Barlow?"

"How did you hear of him?" Chad asked.

"We . . . just did," Bob said. "We didn't mean to, but it just . . . happened. . . . ."

"Chad, do you know anyone named Barry Barlow?" Betty asked.

"Yes," Chad said. "I know him well. All right, Cindy—and you Bob—now that you've involved a friend of mine, let's have the whole story. Maybe we can make some sense of this, though I'm beginning to doubt it."

"We—saw you with him," Cindy said. "We—know what that means."

"Know what it means?" Chad asked. "Maybe you do, but I don't. First, how did you learn his name?"

"We saw it in the newspaper," Bob admitted.

"Oh—yes. I saw that article too. How did you know he was a friend of mine?"

"Because . . . because I saw you in the car with him," Cindy said, "and that night you went out without telling anybody where you were going . . . we saw you meet him."

"Of all the crazy explanations. What did you do, follow me?"

"Not exactly. We knew where you were going to meet him. You mentioned the name of the place over the phone. Bob and I went there and saw you meet him."

"Dad," Bob said earnestly, "it won't make any difference to us. We'll stand behind you, but maybe it's not too late. Maybe . . . whatever you took . . . you can pay back and nobody will know."

"Please, Daddy," Cindy implored. "Whatever you promised him you'd do, don't do it."

"I," Betty broke in, "would love to be far more than an innocent bystander in this exchange of words. Somebody fill me in, please."

Chad's slow grin spread all over his face. "What do you know," he said with considerable feeling.

"That's just it," Betty said. "I don't. I don't know anything. What is this secret between you and Bob and Cindy?"

"I'm not too sure," Chad said, "but I think they suspect me of taking a bribe from this man Barry Barlow. Is that it, kids?"

Cindy nodded. "What else can it be? The newspaper said he was a criminal. That's true, isn't it?"

"Yes, unfortunately, it's too true."

"What on earth are you getting at?" Betty demanded. "No more fooling around. The children accused you of taking bribes, Chad. I know that isn't so, but whatever brought it all on?"

"Before this goes any further," Chad said, "I want to tell all of you a little story. It's not one I'm exactly proud of, though I don't suppose it was much to begin with. What I'm going to tell you is the precise truth. You have to believe it's true to properly understand it."

"We will understand," Cindy declared solemnly. "I promise we will, Dad."

"Won't make any difference to us," Bob reiterated.

"Well," Chad said, "it's nice to be forgiven for something I didn't do, but—here's the story. Barry Barlow and I grew up together. We were real boyhood pals right up until we were fourteen. I can remember that night so well. It was hot and sticky. We were wandering about, broke as usual because our people didn't have any money. We were at a dead loss for something to do when we passed this bakery. We knew it well because we always hoped that someday we'd have enough money to buy something there. The most savory smells always came out the door, and the windows were full of the fanciest looking cakes and pies you ever saw.

"Well, this night we walked past the place and darned if the front door wasn't ajar. Know how we discovered it? By the smell of the bakery. The store was in darkness, the bakery part was shut down because it was a Saturday night and no baking was done for Sunday, so they were closed. All we could think of was the fact that by pushing open that door we could lay our hands on something our stomachs craved, and our brains had conjured up as the greatest food ever created."

"Daddy," Cindy said, "you don't have to do any explaining."

"We don't care about why it happened," Bob added.

Chad nodded. "Thank you, kids, but I have to tell the rest of it. We pushed open the door and we went inside. There was a tray of jelly donuts on the counter. We stuffed them under our shirts, all we could take. But what we didn't know was that the baker hadn't left. He was sleeping in the back room and he must have heard us. He came flying out and we ran for it. Right toward the cop on the beat who happened by. I guess we acted by instinct, knowing that cop could chase only one of us. We split up. I ran uptown, Barry ran downtown. The cop went after him and caught him. He never told who I was, and I got rid of the loot as fast as I could. I did have some trouble trying to explain to my mother how it happened there was about half a pound of jelly inside my shirt."

"That's . . . all?" Bob asked.

"Now wouldn't that be a fine way to end a story? I guess it really began then. Barry was lectured and put on probation. Now I'm not saying this mischief started him on a career of crime, but pretty soon he was in trouble again and this time he was put away. That hardened him, turned him into a man who was determined not to work again, but to take whatever he wanted if he thought he could get away with it. Barry never resorted to violence. He became one of the clever, independent criminals who prey on society without inflicting any physical harm on it.

"So that's it. I became a cop, Barry became a crook. But we stayed friends and we wrote now and then, though that stopped because Barry was afraid someone might hear about it and I'd be embarrassed because I'd communicated with a criminal. Whenever he passed this way, he always looked me up and we had a quiet lunch together, or maybe dinner."

"You didn't tell me about him," Betty said. "Not that it made any difference except that I'd have insisted you bring him home."

"That's why I never told you. Barry wouldn't have it. The one thing he dreaded was getting me into trouble because we knew one another."

"That's all there is to it?" Betty asked.

"That's all. Are you satisfied, kids?"

Cindy rushed to embrace him. "Daddy, I'm so sorry. We had no right to just assume . . . what we did."

"Gosh, Dad," Bob said, "we just couldn't understand it."

"I hope you do now. Barry and I live in completely different worlds, but that doesn't mean we can't be friends. He knows that if he pulled anything here I'd arrest him. When he comes to Los Angeles, he's one of the most law-abiding people on the face of the earth. And I'll add this—he's also the loneliest man I know. He's quit breaking the law. That's what he had to tell me. I'm glad, but I don't trust him to have quit completely. I hope he has. I like him. Now, what brought this on?"

"It was the newspaper article and Mr. Barlow's picture and . . . and . . . you said we were going to have three weeks . . . and we were going to live like millionaires and . . . and, a lot of stupid things," Cindy confessed.

"Well, Chad, you've got to admit she has a point there," Betty said.

"Yes, I admit it. Sort of circumstantial evidence, but I guess I'd have wondered too. So, being more or less convinced I had turned into a bad cop, you kids were willing to back me up. I'm proud of that."

"And I," Betty said, "think it's time to end the suspense and tell us where we're going on this millionaire's trip."

"Deputy Chief Anders has loaned us his houseboat."

"Houseboat?" Bob shouted. "You mean we got a houseboat for three whole weeks?"

"That's what we've got. And I've plans all made to stop every night at some city where there's a fine restaurant where we can dine and dance and generally have fun. By day we can loaf and fish and swim."

"Wonderful," Betty said.

"I can't get over it," Cindy said. "We'll dance every night?"

"Well, every night we tie up at a town big enough to have a good place for dancing. There'll be enough, I assure you."

"And the three weeks?" Betty asked. "How did you manage that?"

"By borrowing the houseboat from a ranking officer who can fix things like that. Besides, I had time coming to me. So you see, we're all set, and I'm going to enjoy this vacation more than any, because I've got a couple of kids I'm real proud of. They were wrong, but they believed they were right and willing to sacrifice the vacation and everything else to help me. Okay—tomorrow we start out and we'll make it the best vacation ever."

"I've got to pack," Cindy said. "I was such a nut that I didn't even start because I didn't think we were going."

"Heck, I can pack in ten minutes," Bob said happily.

Brian clattered downstairs and came into the room wearing his raincoat, the pockets of which bulged to their very limit.

"I'm ready," he announced, "but I got to wear my raincoat because I have to carry stuff in the pockets I couldn't get in the suitcase and the paper bags I had, so I'm going to wear the raincoat. . . . ."

"You can wear anything you like," Chad said. "Tonight you've caught a happy man at his best."

Cindy paused at the door and looked back. "Daddy?"

"Yes, Cindy."

"I'm glad you ran uptown."

Chad nodded. "Yes, so am I. Mighty glad."

THE TIN BOX

Detective Sergeant Chad Smith looked up from his dessert, studied his family for a moment and laid down his spoon.

"All right," he said, "let's have it. Why are you all staring at me? Why the lack of conversation tonight? Usually I can't get a word in no matter how hard I try, what with Bob talking about football, Cindy talking about dates and dresses, and Brian talking about anything that enters his head. To say nothing of my wife who does her share."

"We've been waiting for you to tell us what's on your mind," Betty Smith said. "You're the one who's been quiet."

"Yeah," Brian, seven years old, said. "We got your favorite dessert—ice cream and butterscotch—and you never said a word. It's mine too. I like it."

"You haven't spoken a word since we sat down to eat," Cindy commented.

"Proof there's something important on your mind," Bob added. He was fifteen and believed he possessed a mature slant on things, especially family matters.

"So that's it." Chad Smith resumed eating his dessert. "Well, this is my favorite dessert. Roast beef is my favorite dinner. I even like carrots—and you should take a lesson from that, Brian. Do I have to gab all during the meal like a one-man sewing circle?"

Betty smiled and shook her head in reproof. "It's no use, Chad. You might as well tell us."

Chad compressed his lips for a moment and gazed at his family with as much sternness as he was capable of showing, which wasn't much.

"Got so a man's inner soul is revealed every time he sits down to eat with his family. What's on my mind is of no importance to any of you. It's police business."

"No, Chad, you can't get away with it. You've worked on police business of great importance and never showed a sign of worry. This may be police work, but it's also personal and, if it is, we should share in it."

"If you don't finish your dessert," Brian said, "may I have it, Dad?"

"No, you'll get too fat. All right—I guess it is personal and police too. Brings me way back . . . too far back. Something happened today to bring it into the present. Cindy, you might oblige me by warming my coffee. Well, this afternoon I had a call to make and I enlisted the services of a rookie cop to drive me. It was an arrest on a warrant and I couldn't drive and handle a prisoner too. Anyway, when I served the warrant the prisoner took off like a shot. He got to the street and ran down the sidewalk. I could have picked him off easily but this wasn't a felony charge and I wasn't about to shoot a man because he committed a minor crime."

"Oh, Chad, don't tell me your rookie cop shot him?" Betty asked.

"My rookie cop stopped him, but he didn't shoot him. He ran to the police car, took out a nightstick which he carried in it. He wound up like Vida Blue, sent that club skidding down along the sidewalk. It hit the running man's ankles and knocked him flat on his face. He couldn't even get up until we helped him."

"Gosh, that was some trick," Bob said. "Are you able to do that?"

"No—I never could, but I once knew a man who was an expert at it. That's why this rookie brought it all back."

"So what's the harm in that?" Cindy wanted to know.

"It's something I'd rather I didn't remember," Chad said. "That's all I'll say about it now. Seems we've finished dinner and it's assignment time for dishes. Get with it, kids."

Cindy and Bob gathered dishes, carried them to the kitchen. Brian helped but his part of the chore was finished when he delivered his own plates and silver. It was agreed he was too much of a hazard wiping dishes but with the promise that when he was old enough to handle the job, it would be his permanently. Brian was free to go out and play while Chad and Betty sought the temporary seclusion of the living room. Chad picked up the evening paper but scanned the headlines without interest and put it down again.

"You are upset," Betty said. "Want to talk about it now that the kids can't tune in?"

Chad nodded. "It's about an ex-cop named Matt Gilden. When I joined the force he was assigned to teach me the ropes. He was an older man—not by so much, but he had a lot of experience and he was a fine teacher. Anyway, all this happened before we were married, so it's really ancient history. Matt got into trouble. He was filling a tin box."

"Tin box? Do you mean he was taking bribes?"

"That's right. It was an expression we used in those days for cops on the take. Matt had a big one and he crammed it full according to all the evidence at hand. I can tell you I was never more surprised in my life. Matt was one man I'd never suspect of that."

"What's this to do with the rookie cop?"

"Matt was an expert in using a nightstick that way. I never knew anyone else who could do it as well, and this kid—this rookie—used Matt's technique. He was so good at it I wondered if Matt could have taught him."

"Is it such a fine art, this method of pulling down a running criminal?"

"You bet it is. Takes more practice than I'd be willing to give it. The rookie couldn't have just picked it up. He had to get taught."

"So what if that happened, and your old friend with the tin box did teach him?"

"The rookie would be tainted. Mind you, he is likely as good a man as anyone and will make a fine police officer, but if he's associated with Matt Gilden, there are a lot of old timers who'll remember."

"That was years ago," Betty said. "Do you carry a grudge that long?"

"No, not ordinarily, but in Matt's case I'm afraid the memory sticks. With me and plenty of others. It wasn't the fact that he accepted money, it was the way he did it. With the most cold-blooded deliberation I ever saw in a criminal. He should have gone to prison. He didn't, and that rankles some too, because he'd put many a man there for doing the same thing. He was fired from the force, but there wasn't enough evidence to stand up in court. He didn't fight it. He just pulled out and disappeared."

"I still say after all these years you should have softened, darling."

"Yes, I know. I guess I was too young and too impressionable. I held Matt up as if he were an idol. I wanted to fashion my whole career after him—and he let me down with a bang I can't forget."

"You haven't seen him since?"

"I've never wanted to."

"What will you do about this rookie, Chad?" Betty asked.

"Nothing. He's not to blame for what happened before he was born. Even if Matt Gilden trained him, was his friend, even a relative, that has nothing to do with Patrolman Chris Foster. I'm going to forget it. Partly because I don't think Matt is implicated. He said he was leaving town and I think he did."

"Good," Betty said. "Now you've got that out of your system, Sergeant Smith, you can pay attention to your family again. Cindy needs a new ball gown for a college dance."

"Okay, we can afford it."

"This one serves a double purpose. It's a long formal worn over hot pants. The skirt comes off. It's - daring, if that's the word."

"Ought to look mighty nice on her."

"Good heavens, do you approve?" Betty asked in amazement.

"Certainly, I do. She has the figure for it. She's young, she's attractive. If she wants to show off, good luck to her."

"I'll break it to her gently. This she didn't expect. I'm not sure that I wholly approve. . . . ."

Chad looked up to find his youngest son staring at him from the doorway. "How long have you been standing there?" he asked.

Brian, his face as serious and woebegone as Chad had ever seen it, walked slowly up to his parents. "Dad, if you hurt Mr. Gilden, I'll never talk to you again as long as I live."

"Oh, my," Betty said, "he's been there for some time."

"Brian, do you know a man named Matt Gilden?"

"Yes, sir. He's my friend and you can't hurt him. I won't let you."

"Come here, son. I'm not going to hurt your Mr. Gilden. I know you heard us talking about this man I once knew, but your Mr. Gilden just happens to have the same name."

"His grandson is named Chris. He's my friend too."

Chad whistled softly. "Might not be such a coincidence after all. Where can I find your Mr. Gilden, Brian?"

"I won't tell you. You can't make me tell you. He's my friend. I won't tell."

Brian whirled about and raced out of the room and out of the house, slamming the door behind him.

"Whew," Chad said, "we really bit one off that time."

"It must be the same man," Betty said. "I don't know how Brian met him. He never mentioned him that I can recall."

Chad raised his voice. "Bob . . . Cindy . . . come here for a minute, please."

Cindy, wiping damp hands on her apron, came in first looking worried. She shot a swift glance at her mother.

"No, dear," Betty said, "it's not about the gown. Your father approves. This is another matter."

"Oh Dad." She flew to him and hugged him. "You aren't an old stick in the mud after all."

"Stick in the mud?" Chad said. "That's an old-fashioned expression from a young 'un like you."

"You're a darling," she said in an ecstasy he found delightful.

Bob entered with many inquiring glances at his father. Chad settled back in the chair. "Brian heard your mother and I discussing a police officer who was fired for taking bribes. It seems Brian knows him, even knows the rookie I was with today. Names were mentioned—the ex-cop is

Matt Gilden. The rookie is Chris Foster. Did either of you ever hear of them?"

"Pop Gilden," Bob said in an amazed voice.

"We know Pop," Cindy broke in before Bob could elaborate. "I guess we've always known him. Or it seems that way. He runs a candy and magazine store near Silas Jones Elementary school where Brian goes now, and where Bob and I used to go."

"I recall mention of a candy store owner named Pop," Betty said, "but I don't think anyone ever spoke his last name."

"Everybody knows him as Pop," Cindy said. "Dad, he's a fine man. He's a wonderful man."

"He's been in the neighborhood all these years and I never knew it," Chad marveled. "It doesn't seem possible."

Betty said, "You'd have little reason to ever go that way."

"But I used to pick up the kids. I don't remember the candy store, but it must have been in plain sight."

"Why would you be interested in a little neighborhood store? You barely know where the supermarkets are these days."

"Imagine it," Chad said. "Practically breathing down the back of my neck all these years and probably laughing his head off at my ignorance of his whereabouts."

"What's he done to you?" Bob asked.

"Let's not talk about that while I'm still in a state of shock," Chad said. "The subject is dropped. That's official. I'd better go out and find Brian. I think he was considering running away."

"He'll be on the back porch," Betty said. "That's where he runs away to."

"Come on," Bob said to Cindy. "Back to the grind. We're not privileged people around here."

"Just one thing," Cindy said, "Pop has been a friend to all of us—all the kids who ever went to Silas Jones Elementary. If a kid has no money, he sells on credit, knowing he'll never get paid, and poor kids get a big sack of candy for a nickel. Pop's been going broke all these years just trying to help kids. I want you to know that because I have a feeling you don't like him and you might be able to do something to him."

"No," Chad said. "I don't hate the man and I can't do a thing to him. It's ancient history. I'll find Brian."

Brian's tear-stained face looked up at his father as Chad sat down on the porch steps beside him.

"I'm sorry I hurt you, Brian," Chad said. "I didn't mean to. Bob and Cindy just explained about Pop. Maybe he's not even the man I used to know."

"I don't care if you did. He's my friend. I owe him a nickel."

"Oh-ho, been running a credit line with him, son?"

"I was busted."

"Now you're worse than busted. You're in debt. Ever think of that?"

"Sure do. Can I have a raise?"

"Certainly. For one week I'll raise you five cents so you can get even."

"That ain't much."

"I wish someone would come along and give me a raise that would clear all my debts, even if the raise didn't last more than a week."

"You got to promise you won't do anything to Pop."

"You have my solemn word."

"Okay. I suppose I got to go to bed now."

"It's getting near that time."

"Okay, long as you promised."

"Come on, let's go. Wash your face in the kitchen before

you kiss your mother good night. Can't let her see that any of us men have been crying."

At mid morning, Chad entered the office of the Captain of Detectives. "Morning," he said. "You busy?"

"Not for you, Chad. What's on your mind?"

"Ummm . . . I don't exactly know how to go about this. First of all I'd like to enter a commendation on the record of a rookie cop named Chris Foster."

"Oh? What's special about him?"

"He's got a trick that should be taught all rookie cops. All of us old-timers too, for that matter. It's the use of a nightstick—throwing it along the sidewalk to bring a running man down."

"This rookie knows how to do that?"

"He's an expert at it. Helped me bring in a warrant arrest yesterday."

The Captain's voice grew more gravelly than usual. "Matt Gilden was an expert in that. It's not an art known to all cops. It was his specialty. Are you telling me this rookie learned it from that . . . that old crook?"

"I pulled the rookie's file. He's Matt's grandson."

The Captain's face grew stormy. "All applicants to the force are investigated. Somebody slipped, somewhere. I'll look into it."

"Hold on, Captain," Chad said. "Before we do anything drastic about this, maybe we ought to look into it ourselves."

"Look into what? Matt took bribes, several thousand dollars. He was a tin box cop and I hate that kind the most. He even admitted it, and didn't offer the slightest defense. He should have gone to prison."

"I know. That's what I thought too, but one thing always bothered me. Matt just wasn't the type to accept bribes. I knew him—very well. He broke me in. I think my surprise at what he did built up my anger against him. I felt cheated, and deceived, and that's all I thought about."

"I still think that way, about any crooked cop."

"After twenty-seven years, hate softens, Captain. At least with me. But I know what this will do to the rookie if it gets out. Through no fault of his, he'll be regarded with suspicion because of what his grandfather did."

"His grandfather taught him that nightstick trick. I wonder what else he taught him."

"So do I. That's why I want permission to talk to the boy."

"For what reason, Chad? There's a question on the application he filled out, asking if anyone in his family had ever been convicted of a crime. You just looked at his file. Did he answer in the affirmative?"

"No, sir, he did not."

"So you think that's a good start for a rookie?"

"He answered the question truthfully. Matt never was convicted. Not even tried in court."

"All right, so it's a point. What are you going to prove by talking to him?"

"I don't know."

"What's Matt doing now?"

"Running a little candy store for kids near one of our schools."

"That's nice. He must be a great influence on our future generation."

"He's going broke there. He's giving his merchandise away."

"He can probably afford it, with all the money that went into his tin box."

"Why the tin box? That's what I want to know. I wasn't aware of it all these years, but it's bothered me. At least it used to. How about it? Can I talk to the boy?"

The Captain leaned forward over the desk. "Listen to me, Chad. Talk to him. Tell him we know about his grandfather, and that what Matt did to the cops in general will wash off on the boy. It's bound to. If he comes up for promotion and that gets out, he'll be turned down. Maybe he won't care, but it'll happen. You know there's nothing hated more than a cop who was on the big take. For the boy's sake, warn him."

"That was the general idea," Chad said. "Thanks. I didn't want to go over your head on this."

"Report back when you finish your investigation. Consider it an assignment on company time." The Captain leaned back now, more relaxed. "You know, Chad, I used to think Matt Gilden was the greatest cop on record. Like you, I guess that's why I hated him when he let us all down. Go ahead, see if you can find out what happened."

Chad returned to his desk, called personally and learned that Officer Chris Foster was off duty. Chad got his phone number and address. He dialed. A woman's voice, soft and gentle, assured him she would call Chris at once.

"This is Sergeant Chad Smith," Chad said when Chris came on the wire. "I'll be driving by your house in twenty minutes. Please be waiting for me outside."

"Yes, sir," Chris replied. He didn't ask a single question. Chad winced as he hung up. Chris was no fool. He had probably guessed what this meeting meant.

In civilian clothes, Chris was a fine looking young man. Sturdy, broad of shoulder, almost but not quite handsome. He got into Chad's car. Chad greeted him and then said nothing until he brought the car to a stop at the curb on Ocean Avenue alongside the colorful park high atop the Palisades of Santa Monica. They got out to walk along the path under the line of palms while the Pacific surged toward the shore below them.

"I take it," Chris said, "you found out."

"Yes, I found out."

"Grandfather said you would. He said you were the smartest cop he ever knew."

"I'm just a detective sergeant, Chris. You didn't mention who your grandfather was in your application to join the force."

"Nobody asked me," Chris declared with a slight grin.

"True enough."

"Are you going to make trouble for him, Sergeant?"

"No, not the slightest."

"Do you know why Grandfather accepted money as a bribe?"

"Why he did it has no bearing, only the fact that he did."

"You're wrong, sir."

"A cop who takes a bribe has no excuse."

"Twenty-seven years ago, how much did a cop make in those days, Sergeant?"

"I lived on it. Got married on it."

"Did you provide expensive medical treatment for your wife on it?"

Chad leaned against a railing and looked out over the Pacific. "I've heard that one before, but go on. I'll listen."

"My grandmother had a kidney condition that resulted in the loss of function. At that time it was like a death sentence, but a method of treatment had been discovered. Something new—a machine that cleaned the blood when the kidneys could not. In those days it was a big, cumbersome affair. There were very few of them, there was a great need for them and to get the use of one required a small fortune in cash."

Chad faced the young man. "I didn't know that. Your grandfather never offered any explanation. It might have been easier on him if he did."

"Grandpop is loaded with pride, Sergeant. You have a lot of it too. I can tell."

"I suppose I have. Get on with it."

"He kept Grandma alive for two years. Two whole years. All he had to do was accept an offer to turn his back and the money to finance it was his. He'd have done anything to keep her alive. Anything at all. This was the only way he could find."

"He could have gone to the credit union. We had one then."

"To get thirty-five thousand dollars in a lump sum?"

Chad whistled sharply. "A fortune in those days. Still, it's no excuse, Chris."

"Of course it isn't. Grandpa knew that. He knew he'd have to pay for it a thousand times over—and he has. People like you saw to that."

"Now hold on," Chad objected quickly. "I didn't even know where he was."

"You didn't have to. Grandpa knew what you were thinking. But he didn't mind too much. In his view, he got a bargain. His wife lived for two more years. For that Grandpa would have paid anything—in money or reputation, or both."

"He could have asked for consideration," Chad argued.

"And have Grandma hear about it? What if he told the reason why he accepted a bribe? Wouldn't the newspapers of those days have had a field day with it? Grandpa, after he was fired, used to go to the hospital wearing the uniform he was no longer entitled to wear. When Grandma was sent home, he kept the uniform in the garage and changed into it before he entered the house. She never knew. He meant that she never would. He worked at it."

"You know, this puts a different light on things, Chris. I don't condone what your grandfather did. Not by a long shot. But I realize that I might do it myself, placed in the same circumstances. It would be a temptation too big to turn down."

"I hope you never have to make that decision, Sergeant."

"Yes. Yes, I hope so too."

"What will you do now? Have me thrown off the force?"

"Nobody ever entertained such an idea. You're going to make a fine officer."

"Thank you. I should. Grandpa had me on the force when I was six years old. He made me toe the mark in school because a cop had to know much more about things than the average man. That's what he used to say. When I was old enough, he scrounged a rule book and copies of old entrance exams. He drilled me into the use of them, he taught me how to shoot, how to fight. I knew Oriental style fighting before it was even heard of here. He taught me how to use a nightstick, like I did yesterday. I had no idea it would give me away, but when I saw the look on your face after we collared the prisoner, I knew what you were thinking."

Chad resumed walking, taking Chris' arm as he did so. "Right now I'm thinking of recommending that you train other officers in the proper use of the nightstick. It's a lost art. I could take some lessons myself."

"Thanks, Sergeant," Chris said softly.

"Don't thank me. I made a serious misjudgment of character in regards to your grandfather. He was my friend and I turned my back on him. Maybe today I wouldn't, but I was young in those days and full of bright honor and respect for the badge. It never occurred to me that there might be a reason behind what happened. And it should have, because I did know your grandfather so well. I should have looked for the reason, but all I could see was the surface and that was nasty to look upon."

"Grandpa learned to live with it, but not easily. He practically banned himself from the rest of the world, except for the kids who patronized his store. He's content now. Worried, to be sure, but he has no regrets. You have to understand that. He did what he did for a purpose he thought was worthwhile. He still thinks so."

"There wasn't a tin box then?" Chad asked.

"I don't get that, sir."

"We call a cop on the take, a cop with a tin box where he kept his pay-off money."

"There was no tin box. This was a one-time thing. He knew he was going to be caught, but he regarded that as part of the price he had to pay for the woman he loved dearly, to live another twenty-four months."

"Would you do what he did, Chris?"

"No, sir. I wouldn't have the guts."

"Come down to it, neither would I. I'll take you home now. There'll be no trouble. When it comes time for promotions—and to you they'll come quickly—there'll be no reference to another cop who sacrificed what he loved best—almost best—to help his greatest love." Chad glanced at his watch. "Say—I only put a nickel in the parking meter. This is Santa Monica. I can't wangle out of a ticket here. Come on."

Chad was whistling as he parked the car in the driveway and walked toward the house. Bob was on his way out, something about a date, Chad gathered. Betty met him at the door as usual and he kissed her fondly.

"I love you very much," he said. "I never believed a man could love a woman more, but I found out today it's possible. Yes, sir, more than possible. A genuine fact. Give you the details later when. . . . ."

He stopped to look at Cindy, slowly and gracefully

approaching him in her new gown. A pale green, right down to the floor, form fitting and Chad had the right word for it.

"Elegant," he said.

"Watch," Cindy said. She manipulated buttons and zippers and the long gown fell away. She stood before him in brief pants. Chad looked at her in wonder.

"I'm responsible for that?" he asked in awe.

"*We* are, darling," Betty reminded him. "Isn't she lovely?"

"I don't know what it means," Cindy said "but I like it coming from you, Dad."

He hugged her, told her to get decent again and held the lower part of the gown for her. They entered the living room. Brian sat in a large chair, knees up to his chin while he studied a magazine so intently Chad knew he wasn't seeing a word on the pages.

"Hi, champ," he said.

Brian didn't look up. "Hi."

Chad said, "How much time before dinner? I know I'm a little early."

"Oh, half an hour. Maybe more. Why?"

"Brian and I have an errand to do. He's in a little financial trouble and I thought I'd straighten it out for him. No questions. A man doesn't have to talk about being remiss in paying a debt. Come on, champ. Let's go see Pop."

A small brass bell tinkled as Chad opened the shop door. The store wasn't large, just enough room for an ice cream dispensing freezer, two long glass enclosed cases for candy and a rack for magazines which proved to be mostly comics.

There were curtains at the rear and they parted as a tall,

ramrod straight man with a great shock of white hair, moved toward them.

"Afternoon, Matt," Chad said. "My son tells me he's on your books for a nickel. I've come to pay it. Nice to see you again."

"Is it, Chad?" he asked.

Chad nodded. "Bank on it, friend. Thanks for giving us a good cop. Chris will make it big. This I know."

"It was one way to repay, Chad."

"You didn't need a way. Here's the nickel and maybe Brian can pick out a sackful. How about it?"

"Oh, boy," Brian began the tedious process of making up his mind between forty assortments of candy.

"Well now," Chad said. "I think I'll take me a dime's worth of that old-fashioned rope licorice. Used to chew it when I was a kid and spit great guns pretending I was chewing tobacco."

"Time for pretending is over, Chad," the old man said.

Chad reached across the counter and took his hand. "Long overdue, friend. Too long."

PATTERN OF GUILT

With one exception, the Chad Smith family living on Primrose Lane was much like any other family of five at dinner time. Chad praised the roast, the potatoes, the vegetables, the salad and the coffee. Betty, his wife, smiled contentedly. Cindy, eighteen years old, still worried about skin blemishes and passed up anything fattening. Bob, fifteen, ate everything in sight with relish and Brian, seven, picked at everything except dessert.

The exception came when Chad Smith glanced at his watch, arose, went to the closet where he kept his service gun. He slipped this into its holster, put on his coat, slicked back his graying hair and returned to the table.

He bent down and kissed his wife on the cheek. He glanced up and grinned at his children. "See you later, tribe."

"You going out again?" Bob asked.

"What's so important you have to be on duty every night—and every day too?" Cindy asked.

"I thought you were going to help me with my racer," Brian complained. "You been going to help me for more'n a week now. Don't you ever stay home any more?"

"Children," Betty said sternly—as sternly as she was capable of, "your father has to keep unusual hours because he's a policeman. You all know that."

"But it's been two weeks," Cindy said.

"It may be two months more," Chad warned them. "Be back before midnight, I hope."

"Gosh," Brian said, as the door closed behind his father, "I'm never going to win that race."

"Now Brian," his mother said, "no adult is supposed to help you make that soap-box racing car. You have to do it all by yourself."

"If you let Dad help it's cheating," Cindy added.

"Gee, all I want is some advice," Brian said.

"Okay," his brother said, "ask me."

"What do you know? Dad's smarter'n you."

"Okay, but ask me anyway."

"If I put big wheels on the front and small wheels on the back will I go faster than if I put small wheels on the front and big wheels on the back?"

Bob looked blankly at his sister and then at his mother. "Why don't you have all four wheels the same?" he asked, finally.

"Because that's how everybody's racer will look. That's why. Anyway, I think I can win because I'll go faster, but I don't know which is which, front or back for the big wheels."

"You better ask Dad," Cindy said. "It's an engineering problem."

Betty shook her head. "I don't know if it's legal to ask this kind of advice from your father. The soap-box derby rules are very plain. Everything must be done by the entrant without help of any kind."

"Well, heck, just to ask a question. . . ."

"Wait until your father has more time," Brian's mother said. "Let's get at the dishes."

"Mom, may I be excused just for tonight?" Brian asked.

"If you have a good reason."

"I got to figure out about the wheels. The derby is only a week from now and I ain't got much time."

"All right, run along. That's reason enough," his mother said.

Brian scampered off to the garage where he was in the process of assembling his racer. Betty attacked the dishes, Cindy dried, Bob put them away. She had, Betty Smith always said, the best dish washing machine in the world.

"Hasn't Dad ever said what's keeping him out every night?" Cindy asked.

"No," her mother replied. "Police business, and policemen can't keep regular hours. You know that."

"It may be so," Bob admitted, "but when a cop works all day and half the night too, he gets the extra time off and Dad hasn't taken any. I think what he's doing nights is on his own."

"Whatever it is," his mother said, "you can be sure it's important. We'll have no more guesses. If he wishes to tell us later, he will. All police business is not public."

But Betty Smith was worried. She'd always tried very hard to keep from dwelling upon Chad's profession, for she'd known from the first that it was a dangerous business, though when they were married twenty-five years ago police work was by no means as risky as it is today. Betty made several trips to the window overlooking the street, just to see if there was any sign of Chad's return.

For two entire weeks now, every night of them, he'd gone out soon after dinner and not returned until nearly midnight. When he did come home he seemed to be tired, as if he'd walked a great deal.

Tonight her fears seemed more severe than ever, perhaps because the kids had talked about it. When Betty felt she could no longer stand the suspense she went to the telephone. First she made sure that Cindy was in her room studying. Brian was still in the garage trying to puzzle out the difference between big front wheels or big back wheels on his racer. Bob had gone out—to the Argo Club, he said, a teenage gathering place approved by everyone.

She dialed police headquarters, asked for the detective bureau and then asked to be connected with Sergeant Goodman.

"This is Betty Smith," she said. "Is Chad there?"

"At this hour? He went home long ago, Mrs. Smith. Didn't he show up yet?"

"Oh yes, he's been home, had his dinner and had to go out. I wondered if he was just behind in his desk work."

"He's not here."

"There's nothing going on that would keep him busy evenings?"

"Not that I know of. You sound worried."

"Oh no," she said as lightly as possible. "No more than any policeman's wife."

"I know what you mean. If he shows up here, I'll have him call you."

"Thank you, Sergeant." She hung up slowly. It was police business that kept him out every night. She knew it—but apparently headquarters didn't. It wasn't like Chad not to confide in her, except when there was something of particular danger going on.

At ten-thirty she heard the sound of someone approaching the door. She hurried to the window in time to see Bob fishing in his pocket for his keys. Betty let him in.

"You're home early," she said. "This is Friday night, isn't it?"

"Hi, Mom. Yeah, it's Friday. Dad home yet?"

"No, not yet. Want some cake and milk?"

"Sure would."

They entered the kitchen where she provided him with a tall glass of cold milk and a large piece of cake. She served herself another piece, thinking, as she did so, that frustrated people like to eat.

"I saw Dad tonight," Bob said unexpectedly.

"Oh!" She tried not to betray her intense interest.

"Yeah . . . I saw him."

"Well, where? And what was he doing?"

"I don't know for sure. He was watching the Argo Club."

"But I thought the club was fully approved by parents and even by the police."

"Just the same, he was standing in a doorway across the street trying not to be seen by any of us, but a car swung around the corner and lighted him up so that there was no mistake. It was Dad."

"Perhaps you'd best stay away from the club until we find out what this is all about."

"Gosh, Mom, there's nothing wrong with the club. Honest! If there was I'd have pulled out long ago. I know a policeman's son has got to sort of be an example for other kids."

"Yes, that's true. But if the club is all right, why is your father watching it?"

"Maybe it's not the club."

She didn't want any more of the cake. She laid her fork down and regarded her son seriously. "I wish you'd explain that last remark, Bob."

"Okay. Skinny says Dad is watching him."

"Skinny?"

"He's one of the kids in the club. Dad arrested him

about six months ago but he got off."

"And this Skinny person thinks your father is watching him?"

"He says Dad's always around when he is. He thinks Dad follows him along the street too, and sometimes stands outside his house until very late."

"What did your father arrest him for? Did Skinny say?"

"Burglary."

"That's a serious charge. Usually they are not let go."

"Well, Skinny was trying to get a suit of clothes for his dad. The way he tells it, his father's been out of work and had a chance to get this job, but he didn't have a decent suit to wear for the interview. So Skinny decided to get him one. He just crawled through a small window of this store. He tripped an alarm and Dad answered it. Skinny gave up right away. He didn't resist or anything, and he admitted what he was trying to do."

"He wasn't using very good judgment, was he?"

"I guess not. Dad put in a good word for him because when Skinny told him what he was after, Dad checked and found it was the truth."

"Yes, he'd do that."

"Skinny said Dad was very kind to him and he can't dig this business of Dad following him all the time. Like he was a criminal or something."

"Maybe he is. Did you ever think of that?"

Bob shook his head. "No sir. Skinny said he made that one mistake and he was lucky to get out of it, and he'll never make another. Anyhow, his dad got the job so the family is in good shape now."

"Perhaps your father is watching someone else, not your friend Skinny."

"Like me, maybe?" Bob grinned impishly.

"I don't think he has to worry about you. In any event

you are not to ask him about this. If he is watching either the club, or Skinny, or anyone else there, he has good reason for it. Agreed?"

"Sure, Mom."

"And you will not tell your sister about it."

"Okay, it's just between you and me. But Skinny sure wishes he'd lay off."

"Bring your dishes to the sink. Fetch yourself a towel. In this house you pay for your milk and cake."

Chad came home two hours later, looking more weary than ever. Betty looked up from her book as he entered the living room and stopped to kiss her firmly. He walked to the closet to dispose of his coat and gun.

"Tough night, darling?" she asked.

"Lots of walking. I'm getting a bit old for it, I guess."

"Nonsense, you could pound a beat again if it was necessary."

He sat down across from her. "I guess so. Bob home okay?"

"He came directly from the club."

"Good."

She put down the book. "What do you think of the Argo Club, Chad?"

"I think it's fine."

"I'm glad to hear you say that."

"The kids who go there are the best. There's only soft drinks, some dancing, a lot of chatter. Sounds like a big tea party sometimes. Voices come out of there as if a big shindig is always going on. Come to think of it, maybe there is."

"You seem to know a great deal about it," she said.

"And you seem mighty interested in that place all of a sudden."

"I am. Bob goes there so often."

"Then relax, because he couldn't be among better kids. Boy, I'm tired."

"But just think of all the overtime they'll have to make up to you when this assignment is over."

He looked at her sharply and then laughed aloud. "You've been a detective's wife too long. You're getting pretty sharp the way you ask questions."

"Well, isn't it overtime?"

"This is not official business. Police business, yes, but it's not an assignment. It's something I'm doing on my own."

"You don't care to tell me anything more, Chad?"

"No," he said somewhat curtly. "I do not."

She arose. "I see. Time for bed."

He arose also and put his arm around her. "You want to know what's keeping me out every night until late. I don't wonder that you're curious. I can't tell you. Except that it's in no way dangerous. It's just a job."

She'd been close to tears but she managed a smile now. "Why can't you tell me, Sergeant Smith?"

"Because I may turn out to be a fool, and if I do I don't want anybody to know it but me."

"I'll be good," she promised, "but I don't know if your son will."

"Bob?"

"He saw you watching the club tonight and Bob's friend Skinny says he thinks you've been shadowing him."

"I must be slipping," Chad said. He abruptly changed the subject. "How is the family otherwise? Now that I'm practically a stranger in my own home?"

"They're fine, except for your youngest son. Brian wants some help in constructing his soap-box racing car."

With his arm around her waist, Chad began moving out of the room, turning off the lights as he did so. "Nothing doing. The rules say the kids can't have any help."

"He knows that. All he needs is advice."

"Well . . . maybe that's okay. . . ."

"He wants to know if he can get more speed with big wheels in front or in back."

"Hmmm . . . that's not a bad question. I think I'll leave early tomorrow night before he asks me."

As he brushed his teeth that night, Sergeant Smith was frowning when he looked in the mirror. Betty heard him muttering to himself.

"Big wheels in front for more speed . . . or in back . . . let's see now . . . need all the traction you can get. . . ."

At breakfast, he shuddered when Brian asked him the question he knew was inevitable.

"I've got to think about it, son," he said. "That's an engineering factor and I'm not up on it, but I'll ask around and see if I can find somebody who has the answers. Okay?"

"The derby is Sunday afternoon. I got to know before then, so I can put the wheels on."

"I'll do my best."

"It's not like I want you to put the wheels on, Dad."

"I know . . . you're legally entitled to ask advice. I'll do my best."

"Okay."

Cindy said, "You look tired, Dad."

"I guess I am. Too much running around. I'm all right though. Being busy keeps a man young. And a woman. Look at your mother."

"Stop the blarney and eat," Betty said. "You're going to be late if you don't hurry."

That afternoon Chad phoned to say he couldn't make it for dinner and not to keep anything hot for him. He sounded as if he was in a great hurry so Betty asked no questions. At dinner Bob maintained silence about the subject of his friend Skinny, until Brian had gone out to the garage to work on the car and Cindy had gone to her room to telephone a girl friend, which would keep her occupied for some time.

"I don't dig it, Mom," Bob said, as they finished putting the dishes away. "Skinny told me this afternoon that he was going to show some friends of his around town. Dad didn't come home for dinner. I think he's following Skinny."

"I don't know whether he is or not, Bob, but if he is you can be assured he has good reason for it."

"Skinny's okay now. I know it, Mom. Gosh, Dad gave him a break before, but now he's hounding him."

"You're not certain he is."

"Well, I'm pretty sure of it and Skinny knows it. You see, Mom, lots of the kids say that if a kid slips somewhere and the cops get him, they never let him alone again."

"You know very well that's not the truth," she said.

"Yeah, I know it. Or I think I do. But it sure looks like Dad is harrassing Skinny now. Otherwise, why does he watch him all the time?"

"I don't know, but I am sure this is not harrassment."

"Try and tell the kids that when they find out. I asked Skinny not to say anything, but he's getting sore and he might. That'll make all the kids think the stories about cops are right. We got to prevent that somehow, Mom."

"There's nothing we can do. This is a matter that concerns your father and no one else. I have never known of him to harrass anyone, least of all a boy who made one slip in his life and turned out well in spite of it."

"You wouldn't ask Dad, huh?"

"No, I would not. It's none of my business, nor of yours. Until he wants to tell us."

"I hope he does, before all the kids turn sour on him and all the other cops. I'm going to the club. Okay?"

"If your homework is done."

"It's Friday night, remember?"

She sighed wearily. "I did forget. All right . . . off with you. Be home by midnight."

"I'll probably beat Dad home," he said.

Bob was right. He came home half an hour before Chad arrived, more tired than ever.

"Tomorrow's my day off and I'm glad," he told Betty. "Don't make a mistake and wake me up, will you?"

"I'll do my best. Chad, I feel I must talk to you."

"If it's about my staying out nights, please don't. I can't even comment. As I told you before, I may be the biggest idiot on earth, but I'll be the only one to know it if I am. A man's got to keep his reputation for good police work up to its peak and being wrong on this case won't help it, believe me."

"Bob says the way you're watching this boy called Skinny, is harrassment."

"He does, eh?"

"He says he's convinced most of his friends that policemen do not harrass anyone, but with Skinny talking about you following him all the time, they're beginning not to believe Bob, and I consider that serious."

"So do I. I wish it didn't have to be that way. Did my genius youngest son solve the problem of the wheels yet?"

"He's still worrying about it."

"I asked around. Nobody has the answer. Not those who didn't think I was crazy, that is. Big wheels in front or big wheels in back." He shook his head. "It's a puzzle. I didn't go far enough in school. Or I had too many kids. Or those I have are smarter than me."

"He'll be looking for an answer tomorrow. May I

remind you of that? It's your day off."

"You don't have to remind me. I think I'll sleep all day."

They made their way to the bedroom. "Is this boy called Skinny actually very thin?" Betty asked.

"With a little effort he might wiggle through the mesh on a tennis racket. They tell me he eats like a team of horses and never puts on a pound."

"If you have occasion to talk to him," Betty said, "ask him how he does it. I got on the scale this morning . . . murder!"

"Dad!"

Chad stopped. "Yes, Bob?"

"Can I talk to you for a minute?"

Chad signaled Betty to keep going. "Okay, if you cut it short. I'm tired."

He entered Bob's room and sat down on the edge of the bed. Bob was propped up, apparently he'd been waiting for him to return.

"I've got to talk to you about Skinny," he said. "I promised Mom I wouldn't, but I have to."

"All right, son. Talk."

"You're shadowing him, aren't you?"

"Yes."

"Why?"

"I can't tell you that."

"Is he in any trouble?"

"Not that I know of."

"Then why are you watching him? Following him?"

"This is not a police matter—yet."

"I don't dig that, Dad."

"You don't have to. All you have to do is accept it."

"What's that mean?" There was a trace of belligerence in Bob's voice.

"Simple. Trust me."

Bob slid down along the propped up pillow. "Good night, Dad."

"Well, do you trust me?"

"Yes, sir."

"Thank you," Chad said. "Good night."

He didn't speak of Bob's reason for calling him into the room and Betty didn't mention it. In the morning, the Smith household seemed to be normal again. Chad was home for that day and, Betty hoped, the night as well. He arose late, relieved to learn that Brian was down the street conferring with one of his contemporaries about the wheels. Chad worked around the yard, enjoying it as he always did. He was proud of his home and his family. To him this was the result of a lifetime of hard work and it was well worth it. Of course the house would need painting next year, and painters were so expensive he'd have to do it himself. Policemen don't make the kind of money that allows them to hire much professional help. He'd get around to the job one day. It could wait for the moment.

Bob was off to join some friends at the club. Cindy had gone to the mountains with Liz Mallard and her family. Chad sank lazily into one of the folding chairs in the back yard, closed his eyes and dozed. It was nice to be home with the right to be lazy. He considered taking Betty out for dinner that night. Cindy would be gone until late. Bob could take care of himself and Brian as well.

Brian! Chad all but leaped out of the chair. He hurried to the garage and found the racing car still in a dozen or more pieces. By the looks of it, the car had been assembled and taken apart a dozen times. He compared the large and the small wheels, considered putting the racer together and testing it out, but that would clearly be an infraction of the rules, even if Brian didn't know about it. Anyway, it would be like him to pop in just as the thing was assembled. Chad withdrew before anything like that could happen.

Betty glowed at the idea of going out to dinner, just the two of them. She immediately proceeded to prepare her bath, lay out an almost new dinner gown, debated whether to wear her fake pearls or her fake emeralds and decided she didn't need either. The fake rubies looked better.

Chad phoned the Argo Club and asked for Bob. "Be home by six," he said. "Your mother and I are going out for the evening. On the town! Alone! You're to take care of Brian. Understand?"

"Sure. Okay, I'll be home in plenty of time."

He was back by five-thirty. Long before his mother was ready. Chad, in his best blue suit, was waiting impatiently, but without comment except to glance at his watch now and then. They were having an early dinner and a theatrical performance at the Music Center Pavilion for which he had secretly managed to secure a pair of good seats on short notice.

"Brian's in the garage working on his puzzle," Chad explained. "I withdrew from the problem on the excuse that I was unable to help him according to the rules. If you should come up with the answers, give him a few hints."

"Okay, but I don't know them any more than you do."

Betty swept into the room, adjusting her wrap. Bob whistled and she walked over to kiss him soundly. "That was nice," she said.

Chad whistled too and she kissed him as well. Then they headed for the door. Before he opened it, Chad came to a halt. "I've got to make a phone call. Bob, see your mother to the car, please."

He dialed, said, "This is Sergeant Smith. Until eight ten I'll be at the Tower Restaurant. By eight-thirty you can have me paged at the Music Center Pavilion. I'll leave word with the ushers. He's home now?"

"Yes, Sergeant. I'm sure of it."

"Fine. Let me know."

"Official business?" Betty asked as he backed the car out of the drive.

"Official," he said.

"We'll be going dancing, I hope?"

"Dancing? Well . . . I didn't make plans for that."

"Then I insist upon something just as exciting."

"I'm home safe," he said. "It'll be a fine evening."

They ate a leisurely dinner at the restaurant thirty-odd stories above the ground, overlooking downtown Los Angeles which, by a miracle of luck, was clear of smog. The evening lights were bright and sparkling. He'd once worked beats over some of the sections far below, and he pointed them out to Betty.

Dessert was being served when Chad was called to the phone. Betty watched him anxiously. A phone call could mean the evening was a disaster. She saw him hang up after only a few words. He immediately made another call.

Chad said, "Bob, I'm going to ask you a question and I want an answer now. Did you tell Skinny I was taking the evening off?"

"Yes, sir," Bob said. "It just came about casually . . ."

"Did he tell you he was going out tonight?"

"I . . . don't want to answer. . . ."

"Son, this is police business now. I demand an answer. Do you know where he's going?"

"Gosh, Dad, I feel like a fink."

"I don't care how you feel. Where is Skinny going? If you know, tell me and be quick about it."

"The Aquarious Ballroom. He's taking a girl."

"That's the swinging joint on Santa Monica Boulevard?"

"Yes. Dad, honest, Skinny's okay. I swear he is . . ."

"Good night," Chad said.

He hung up, hurried back to the table and without sitting down, drank a few sips of coffee and then helped Betty with her wrap.

"Let's go," he said.

"But why the hurry? I was just getting to enjoy the view."

"We'll come back."

"But where are we going in such a rush?"

"You said you wanted to dance, didn't you?"

"Why . . . yes . . . ."

"That's what we're going to do. All evening long. I sincerely hope."

They rode down to the lobby. Chad sent the valet parking attendant for his car, instructing him to hurry. Five minutes later they were speeding up Santa Monica Boulevard in defiance of speed laws.

"You might tell me just where we're going to dance," Betty said indignantly. "It must be an exceptional place if you're in this much of a hurry to get there."

"It's called the Aquarious Ballroom," he said. "Great place. Fine music, lots of lights and noise. Brother . . . you'll be dead for a week. But the dancing is great. If we survive."

He parked the car on the street and led her to the door of the ballroom. It was painted in ripples of pink, pale blue, red and white. When he opened the door, the blast of music made him wince and Betty to draw back. He took her arm in a firm grip and piloted her into the place.

It was well filled. There couldn't have been more than three hundred teenagers here, but they sounded like two thousand. Two rock bands played two different tunes from two sides of the room, but nobody seemed to notice. The floor shook beneath their feet.

Chad paid for two tickets, led Betty to the dance floor and swept her onto it. There wasn't the slightest opportunity to glide into a cozy fox trot or even a rumba. All they could do was study the other dancers and imitate them.

Half an hour later they went to the soft drink bar and consumed something pink that looked deadly but tasted good. Chad wiped perspiration from his face.

"Let's go," he said resignedly, and indicated the crowded floor.

"Not back in that mob," Betty said. "I draw the line, Mr. Smith. Right here. Whatever significance this has—and I know it has some—all bets are off. If I go on that floor again, I'll age ten years in one night. I'm not up to it."

"I guess I'm not either," he said. His eyes kept roving the crowd. Betty saw him rivit his attention on a couple who were flinging their arms about indiscriminately. Especially the young man, for his arms were much longer than average and his thin frame seemed to twist so sharply during the dancing that Chad winced. It was like looking at a human corkscrew.

"And that," Betty said softly, "is Skinny, isn't it?"

"That," he agreed, "is Skinny. I'd say he is aptly named."

"And our evening out meant that we were going to spend our time watching him. How could you, Chad?"

"I took a chance he'd stay home. He's been on the go every night for two weeks and I figured tonight he'd stay in and take care of his kid sister. I know he was supposed to, but then I got this phone call from a neighbor who agreed to watch him and let me know if he left the house."

"How did you know he'd be here? If I may ask such a question."

"I called Bob and asked him. Seems Bob told Skinny this afternoon at the Argo Club that I was taking you out tonight. So when I learned Skinny had changed his plans and dated a girl to come here, I had to come here too."

"I heard about half of that with all this din," Betty said, "but I don't understand any of it."

"You will," he assured her.

"How long will we stay here?"

"Until Skinny decides to go home—or to wherever he has a mind to go."

"Here?" she asked in dismay. "He might stay for hours."

"Shall I see if I can get some cotton for your ears?"

"Let's dance," she said. "If we make some of this noise, we might not notice the rest of it so much."

"Swing it, Mom," he said with a grin. "You were worried about your weight this morning."

By midnight they confined all activity to leaning against the soft drink bar. The dancing hadn't stopped for a moment. It was almost one when Chad led Betty to a phone booth. It was the fifth time he'd made a call from it. This time he emerged with a broad grin on his face.

"We can go home now, Mrs. Smith. We can go home, soak our feet, rub our shoulders with liniment, discuss old age, and fall into bed."

"Not without a full explanation," Betty said. "I'll stay here until you promise, and make you dance all night."

"I promise," he said. "Besides, we have to go to the soap-box derby tomorrow morning. It would break Brian's heart if we missed it."

"I think," she said, "if we go, he'll have to haul me in his racer. I won't be able to walk."

Chad was driving, singing and alternately whistling all the way home. "You're mighty cheerful after an evening like this," Betty observed.

"Reason to be, my dear wife."

"May I share the secret?"

"You may. I didn't make myself out a fool. Full explanation when we get home."

Chad rousted Bob and Cindy out of bed, asked them to come to the living room. Betty, shoeless, with her feet on a chair, waited for them.

Chad said, "This is what it was all about. Skinny arrested by me, some time back, for squirming through a mighty small window to commit a burglary. The window was so small it wasn't believed necessary to shield it with bars of steel or with mesh. I did what I could for Skinny and he got off lightly. I had faith in him, but about a month ago, a series of burglaries took place. Bad ones—jewelry stores, gun shops . . . the loot ran into the thousands. All the burglaries were committed by somebody thin enough to squirm through more of those small windows, and everything pointed to our friend Skinny. I prevailed on the Captain not to haul him in and in return I'd watch him every night."

"Dad," Bob said, "Skinny didn't burglarize any of those places. I know it."

"Can you prove it?" Chad asked.

"Well . . . no . . ."

"I can. After tonight, I can prove it, because I watched Skinny every night waiting for another burglary of this type to take place. If I knew where Skinny was when the job was pulled, then it couldn't be Skinny. You dig?"

"Gosh!" Bob exclaimed. "Yeah, I dig."

"Tonight another job was pulled. We'll get the thin one who did it yet, but Skinny is in the clear. Absolutely."

"You gave up all your nights for two weeks just to follow Skinny so you could prove he was innocent?" Cindy asked.

"Certainly. I'm a cop. My job is to protect the innocent as well as arrest the guilty."

Cindy rushed to him and kissed him. "I guess that'll teach us not to wonder what you're doing when you don't come home."

"But suppose Skinny was guilty. Suppose he pulled a job right under my nose. What an idiot I'd have been. That's why I wouldn't tell anyone. Skinny, however, lived up to the faith I had in him. Someone else knew all about the way he got into that clothing store that night and decided to profit by it. All we have to do is look for a skinny young man. Now go to bed, you two. Tomorrow we attend the soap-box derby so get your voices in shape to cheer your heads off."

Chad reached a hand toward Betty. "I think it's time we old folks retired, darling."

"You go," she said. "I can't get up. Of all the agony a cop's wife must endure, this was the limit."

"Oh, it wasn't such a bad evening," he said.

"Speak louder, my dear. I have a ringing in my ears, like two rock bands going at the same time."

Betty was still stiff the next day, but at the soap-box derby she raised her voice as high as anyone else while she urged Brian on. The cheers turned into groans when the front left wheel fell off and the racer skidded to an ignominious halt.

"Oh, well," Chad said, "he didn't do so badly after all."

"He lost, didn't he?" Bob said.

"Sure—but the twelfth car crashed before Brian's wheel fell off, so at least he wasn't last. Come on, we'll pick up some ice cream cones and console him. Too bad, though. He had the big wheels on the front and we never did find out if that was the answer."

TARGET

"The millennium," Sergeant Chad Smith said, "has reached us."

Betty Smith, his wife and the mother of the brood gathered at the dinner table, looked at him questioningly, not understanding. Chad Smith pointed to the empty plate before his seven-year-old son, Brian.

"He ate everything and never made a squawk."

Betty Smith regarded her youngest son sternly. "All right, Brian. What do you want? What favor are you going to ask?"

Brian, studiously somber, said, "Mom, I was just hungry. . . ."

"You ate carrots, green beans," his sister Cindy remarked. "He sure wants something."

"Maybe he was plain hungry," Bob Smith said. He was fifteen and tended to stick up for his younger brother on occasion.

"Young man," Betty said, "I asked you a question."

"Come on, son. Out with it," Chad urged. "Maybe we're not as bad as you think and we might say yes."

"I want to go camping Saturday."

"Where?" Chad asked.

"Big Bear. That's not so far away. I won't get homesick, honest."

"Who with?"

"Billy Devore and his brother Paul."

"Let's see now," Chad said, "Billy is eight, his brother is how old. . . . . ?"

"Oh, he's all grown up," Brian said hastily.

"He's fourteen," Bob said.

"The answer," Chad said, "is no."

"Oh, gee, we can take care of ourselves. I never get to go no place."

"No! Too many get lost in those mountains. The Sheriff's Department is forever hauling them off ledges and cliffs, using helicopters and dogs. Nothing doing. You can't go."

"Aw, Dad. . . . ."

"You heard what your father said," Betty admonished him. "If he'd given his permission, I'd have countermanded it. He's right. Too many kids get lost."

"I don't go no place," Brian complained again. "Always stay home. A guy gets sick of that. I'll be careful. . . ."

"Once more," Chad said, "the answer is negative. That's all. Now . . . do we have any more problems this evening?"

Cindy shook her head. "I sure got one. I have to turn in a theme on social consciousness by next Monday. It's the major theme of the semester and I haven't even got a subject."

"It ought to be easy," Chad said. "There is enough social significance floating around these days."

"Dad," Brian said, "I promise I'll. . . ."

"No! How many times do I have to tell you?"

"Aw . . . may I be excused?"

"Since you've eaten everything, yes, you may be excused," his mother said.

Brian pushed his chair back, bounded to his feet. "It wasn't worth it, eating all that junk. I never get to go no place. You always say no."

He marched out of the dining room with all the dignity his seven years could muster. Betty sighed and went to fetch the coffee.

"Trouble is, Dad," Cindy said, "everything's been done. Halfway houses, narcotics, run-down sections. . . . It'll be done again a couple of hundred times. I want something original."

"Just keep your eyes open," Chad said. "The subject matter is all around you."

"We got one right here," Bob said. "A kid who isn't allowed to camp out."

"Be quiet!" Cindy said. "I'm serious. I've got to find something different."

"Oh, well," Chad helped himself to another piece of cake. "We all have problems. You should share some of mine."

"A detective has more problems than the next guy?" Bob asked.

"A thousand more. Seems that way sometimes. Especially today."

Betty looked up, always interested in anything out of the ordinary that happened to Chad in connection with his police work. "What happened, Chad?"

"I wasn't going to say anything about it. One of those things."

"For instance," Betty prodded.

"I was driving along Fountain Avenue this afternoon. I saw a teenager come barreling out of a small neighborhood jewelry store with the owner after him and yelling his head off. I stepped on it to try and overtake the kid, but he ducked down an alley so I stopped the car and went after him. It was a blind alley and he was trying to climb the fence at the end of it. I called out for him to surrender or I'd shoot. I had my gun drawn. At the time I didn't know he was a teenager, but when he was hanging on that fence and looked around at me I knew he was just a kid. Not only that, I recognized him. He climbed the fence faster than a cat goes up a tree—and he was gone. Leaving me standing there with my gun leveled."

"You could have shot him?" Bob asked in awe.

"He was a wide open target. It would have been easy, but cops don't shoot at people without more provocation than that. I didn't even know what he'd done. Turned out if I had shot him, I'd have been justified. He'd grabbed two wrist watches from the store worth enough to make it a felony."

"I'm glad you didn't shoot him," Betty said. "He must have had the daylights scared out of him."

"I imagine," Chad said. "That's one of the bad moments of my job. You have to make up your mind in half a second whether or not to pull the trigger. You get bawled out if you do and bawled out if you don't. He could have killed somebody in that store. He might have been armed and dangerous. I took the chance he wasn't."

"You said you knew him," Cindy said.

"Yes—a kid named Wally Toland. He's been in mild jams before. Mostly because he was running around with a gang—the Rathole Gang. They give themselves glorifying names, don't they? Rathole Gang."

"What will you do about him now?" Betty asked.

"No use going to his home. If he is there, they'll say he

isn't. His folks aren't among our better law-abiding citizens. So I'll just pass the word and keep my own eyes open. He'll surface sooner or later."

"I still say I'm glad you didn't shoot him." Betty began gathering the dishes. "Come on, crew, let's get these out of the way."

Chad drifted into the living room where he scanned the newspaper. A glance at his watch told him it was time Brian was safely home, so he wandered out to the front yard to look for him and to see how a recently planted rose bush was coming along. It looked dried out to him but he decided to give it more time.

Brian was seated on the back porch steps, chin resting against his knees, a woebegone expression on his face. He didn't look up as his father approached.

"Time to consider bed, champ," Chad said.

"Why?" Brian asked.

"To get the rest you need, that's why."

"I don't get to go camping?"

"You heard what I said before."

"Then what do I have to be rested up for anyhow? Hanging around here? I don't have to be rested for that. Gosh, Dad, you just don't see things the way I do. Now camping out will help to make me strong. I'll learn how to cook . . . we're bringing a lot of hot dogs. . . ."

"You're not going. That's final. Get in the house and no more arguments. Come Saturday, I'll show you how to cook a hot dog. Right here in the back yard."

"Aw, what fun is that?"

"In the house, champ, before I take my billy club to you."

"Dad, do you carry a billy club?" Brian's interest switched abruptly with this brand new topic.

"No, I don't. I used to when I was on a beat, but a detective doesn't carry one. Any more questions?"

"Yeah, can I. . . ?"

"No!"

"Okay. I guess I know when I'm licked. But you'll be sorry some day when I have to know what it's like in the woods. I never even saw a bear 'cept in the zoo."

"I hope you never do, son."

"Aw, they don't look so mean."

"Take a good look at me and you'll see a bear who *is* mean. Git!"

Brian fled. Chad examined the bush again, sighed over its probable demise and then he went into the house and read the newspaper. Cindy hurried to the door, stopping long enough to ask permission to use the car for a little while.

"Where you going?" Chad asked.

"Oh—just out. To see some friends."

"Okay. Be home by ten. Tomorrow's a school day and there's that theme. Got any ideas yet?"

"I've thought of a good one, Dad. Never been done before. Thanks for the car."

Betty sat down wearily. "Soon Bob will be old enough to drive, and then what happens?"

"We get another car for him, that's all. Maybe one the two of them can share."

"You'll have to make lieutenant if we're going to afford it."

He reached over and patted her hand. "My sweet, I'll probably be Deputy Chief by then. We'll worry about it when the time comes." He paused and reflected a moment. "You know, I'm glad I didn't shoot at that kid. I don't think he's really bad, just gone wrong because nobody's ever given him a break."

"Chad Smith, if you're thinking about bringing another one of those . . . those wild teenage criminals into this house. . . ."

"I never gave that a thought. I merely remarked I'm glad I didn't shoot him. But I might have made a mistake at that. He could now believe he can't get caught and try something else. I hope I don't see him when he does."

The phone rang shortly after nine. Betty handed Chad the phone. "For you. Headquarters."

Chad said, "Thanks. Hello! Yes . . . yes, I know about it."

Betty stood beside him, hands clenched tightly into fists. A night call like this could mean trouble. The worst kind. She wondered how many times in her married life she'd waited like this, taut and full of fear.

"I turned the report over to Detective Rankin yesterday. Nothing to it. He's writing it up, that's why you couldn't find it in my file."

Betty slowly relaxed and went back to her chair, hoping that Chad hadn't noticed. He hung up and finished the newspaper.

"I've been thinking," he said. "Wasn't that a rather abrupt decision of Cindy's? To go out to see friends? She usually saves that for the week-end."

"Well, she did a lot of telephoning before she made up her mind, so she's probably got something to talk about with some of the girls. I don't worry about Cindy."

"Well, neither do I but sometimes you can't help but be a little curious about what the kids do on their own. What about my decision not to let Brian go camping? Do you think it was all right?"

"He's much too young to be with other boys not much older than himself."

"That's about how I had it figured. He was mighty disappointed."

"If that's the greatest disappointment he ever gets in life he'll be lucky."

Cindy returned early but didn't elaborate on where she'd been and Chad didn't ask her. Cindy was eighteen and should be allowed to do what she wished without questioning every move.

Chad did wonder, mildly, next evening when Cindy finished her dinner in a hurry, talked Bob into helping with the dishes without her, and then asked for the use of the car again.

But she returned early once more, went to her room and Chad heard her typewriter going busily until quite late. He decided her expeditions were in relation to the theme she was working on and the whole thing quite innocent.

Next afternoon, Chad arranged to pick up Cindy at the dentist's office and drive her home. She chattered happily as he drove. Chad stopped for a light, pulling up beside a somewhat battered old car. Cindy waved to the driver.

"Hi, Freddie."

The teenager, a rather scruffy looking character with untidy long hair, gave her a casual wave. Chad didn't say anything until both cars were moving again.

"I didn't know you were acquainted with Freddie Leland."

"Oh, just casually. He's not exactly a friend."

"I should hope not," Chad said. "He's not the sort of young man I want my daughter to be going out with under any circumstances."

"Dad, I don't go out with him and I never will. I don't like him."

"How'd you meet a young hoodlum like that?"

"Through a friend. Honestly, he doesn't mean a thing to me."

"I'm glad of that. You want the car again tonight?"

"If I may, please. Just this one more time."

"Thesis work?"

"Yes, it's coming beautifully."

"Good. You may have the car."

"Thanks, Dad. I'll be back by nine."

"Want to tell me about the theme?"

"Not until I'm finished. I think you're going to love it."

"With that kind of enthusiasm I guess your professor will too."

"I only want you to approve. And don't ask me any questions."

Once again she prevailed on Bob to take over the dish washing chore alone. At ten o'clock she wasn't back. Chad went to the window to look out, as if that would bring the car around the corner and into the driveway.

"Cindy is worrying you," Betty said. "Why, Chad? There has to be a reason."

"I don't know. Maybe because she says so little about what she's been doing. Whom she sees. I take it she's been asking questions about this theme she's developing."

"But isn't that the only way she can get her information?"

"Yes, but remember this is a theme about social matters—the poor, the oppressed, all that sort of thing. She may have met up with some characters I wouldn't want her to be seen with."

"Oh, Chad, Cindy has always taken great pains about the type of people she associates with."

"I know that, but she might not consider the ones she interviews for this theme as out of the ordinary."

"You fret too much," Betty said.

"Maybe I have reason to. This afternoon she waved and spoke to a young man I happen to know is a thief and liar. She acted as if they were friends, but she wouldn't elaborate on it except to make it all sound very casual."

"It must have to do with the theme."

"Whatever it has to do with, I don't like it. She's out too late right now. She said she'd be home early. Betty, I'm going do do something I've never done before. I'm going to violate Cindy's privilege of privacy. I'm going to her room and see if I can find out what she's written on this theme."

"If you believe it necessary," Betty said.

"I do. Be down in a few minutes."

He hurried to Cindy's room. To find what he wanted was a simple matter, for there was an unfinished page in the typewriter and a thin sheaf of typed pages on the desk beside it. Chad read most of the first draft of the theme. He put the papers back and stood there in thoughtful silence for a few moments.

Downstairs he went directly to the closet where he kept his jacket. He took down his gun, slipped it into the holster attached to his belt, added handcuffs. He drew on his jacket.

"What is it, Chad?" Betty asked. "If you're going to look for Cindy, do you need a gun for that?"

"It's a departmental rule. All cops carry their guns at all times. I've got to use the phone. Come on, I'll fill you in the best I can. Cindy picked up the story I told about not shooting that boy. She's turning the subject into her theme, making the basis for it a question as to whether or not I was right in not cutting him down."

"She's seeing that boy?" Betty asked in horror.

"She's seeing somebody. The dope she's put on those pages didn't come from her imagination." Chad picked up the phone and dialed. "Lieutenant, this is Sergeant Smith. Have the nearest radio car pick me up at my home as fast as it can get there, and take it off routine patrol for the time being. I'll be waiting out front."

"Is it as serious as that?" Betty asked.

"I don't know. Cindy can take good care of herself, but she may be out of her element with these kind of kids."

"How can you find her? You don't know where she goes or whom she sees. Chad, hurry. Please! Bring her back safely. And don't be harsh with her. She's doing what she thinks is right."

"I'm proud of her," Chad said. "It takes real guts to search out a story like this among the kind of people who are involved. I just don't want her hurt. I'll call you at the first opportunity."

Red lights were already flashing through the window as a radio car responded. Chad hurriedly kissed Betty, told her again not to worry and he raced out to where the car waited. It roared away with screaming siren. Betty returned to the living room, fighting to hold back the tears.

As a detective's wife she should be used to this, but tonight her daughter was involved. Chad would have minimized the danger so that she wouldn't worry too much, but the way he requested the use of a radio car indicated just how dangerous this might be for both Cindy and her father.

Chad instructed the driver to head clear across town and keep the siren open. When he neared his destination, he had the siren and the red lights cut off.

"Stop at the next corner," he told the driver. "Shut off your lights, but keep the motor running. Wait—that's all. Just wait! If you hear any shots, call in for assistance before you investigate, and then be very careful. This may mean nothing, or it could be highly dangerous."

"Okay, Sergeant. It'll be exactly as you say."

"Good. Chances are I'm anticipating too much trouble. With luck there won't be any."

"Yeah," the driver said, "but lately we cops don't have much of that kind of luck."

"I know what you mean," Chad said grimly. "This time I'd better have it."

He rounded the corner, first stopping to survey the empty streets in all directions. This was not a neighborhood where one went walking after dark. He proceeded down the street to the next corner. There he saw his own car at the curb, locked and unmolested.

He knew exactly where he was going, thanks to the details in Cindy's half finished theme. The Rathole Club was in the basement of an old tenement house now waiting to be torn down as part of a reclamation project. Most of the ancient tenements on the block were also empty and ready for the wrecker's swinging ball.

Two young men, evidently on watch at the top of the outside stairs, trotted down them as Chad approached. When he turned toward the steps leading to the basement door, they blocked his way.

"This is private property, mister," one of them said.

They were about eighteen, tough, uncompromising, sure of themselves with that brazen show of force that intimidated so many people. Chad regarded them with open contempt.

"This is city property and you've no business on it. I know about the club maintained in the basement and I'm going in. I'm a police officer. If you have any objections, make them now."

"Show us," one said.

"With pleasure," Chad said. He seized the young man by the coat, hustled him down the steps to the door, banged on it with his free fist and paid no heed to the second man who had followed them.

The door opened two inches. Chad swung his prisoner around so he might be recognized. "This man says I can't come in. I say I can. Want to argue about it?"

"Fuzz," the second youth shouted from behind Chad.

"That's right," Chad said. "The fuzz. Only this time, I'm not here as a cop. My daughter is inside and I'm going in."

The door was opened, reluctantly, but the quality of Chad's anger impressed the doorkeeper with the idea that if he didn't admit this man the door was coming down.

Chad found himself in a dimly lighted cellar room that smelled of dampness and stale tobacco smoke. He didn't detect any odor of burned marijuana. It was a strange table he looked upon. Cindy, cool and unafraid, sat at a rickety table taking notes. Two young men sat close by her, evidently giving her the information she needed. Standing in a shadowy corner was a spindly young man Chad recognized as Wally Toland, whom he had last seen in the sights of his gun as Wally scrambled over an alley fence. Chad showed no recognition of him.

"Dad." Cindy cried out. "Dad . . . oh, why did you have to break this up? I'm all right."

"I can see that," Chad said. He nodded to one of the young men at the table. "Hello, Freddie."

"Hi, Sarge," Freddie said. He didn't look any neater than he had when Chad saw him at the wheel of a car beside his own. "Good-bye, Sarge," he added.

Chad pulled out a chair and sat down. There were seven young men in this room besides Wally and Freddie. They all closed in, forming a tight circle around the table. Chad paid no heed to them.

"I'm taking my daughter home," he said quietly.

"Sarge, she wants to talk to us. . . . ."

"After she finishes talking to you," Chad said. "I'm not here as a cop. I told you that. I'm here as a father."

"You got a warrant or something, you can hassle us. If you ain't, this is our club and we got a right to say who stays here."

"Invite me," Chad said with a wry grin.

"Dad, it's all right," Cindy said. "These boys have been wonderful to me."

"Listen, Sarge. She came in here walking nice and straight and not scared one bit. She told us what she wanted and we said okay, we'd rap. Only thing she didn't tell us was her old man was a cop."

"You found that out when she recognized you this afternoon while I was driving her home."

"Yeah. But she admitted it and said it didn't make any difference."

"Besides," one of the others youths broke in, "when she saw Freddie, she said hello right away."

"Yeah," Freddie agreed. "She was friendly, so we decided not to give her a hard time. Hey, Sarge, did you really have Wally under your gun?"

"Yes, I drew on him."

"Why didn't you shoot?"

"I think my daughter has probably told you that."

"We want to hear it from you, man," Freddie insisted.

"I wasn't sure if he had committed a crime, nor what degree of crime it was, if he had committed one."

"That the only reason?"

"No." Chad looked around. "You guys writing themes too?"

Freddie's thin face grew grim. "I asked you a question, Mr. Smith."

"I notice you are now calling me mister."

"You said you were here as a father and not a cop. You did say that?"

"Yes, and it's true. I didn't pull the trigger because I recognized Wally and I knew how old he was. Cops don't go around shooting kids."

"Listen to him!" someone said sarcastically.

"If I hadn't known how old Wally was I might have pulled the trigger. A cop can't ask for an I.D. Card before he shoots. Especially if the guy he's facing holds a gun too."

Cindy closed her notebook with a snap. "Dad, it's no use. Maybe I've got enough to finish the theme. I don't know, but these boys aren't going to tell me anything more. Not after the way you broke in on them."

"I just came to take you home," Chad said mildly. "All questions, and this controversy, were raised by your friends, not me. Finish asking your questions, take your notes and when you've finished I'll drive you home."

Freddie said, "You carrying a gun now, Mister Smith?"

"Yes."

"That don't make you seem like you're just a father coming here to take your kid home."

"I have to carry a gun at all times. You know that."

"He's right, Freddie," another boy said. "I read in the papers a cop has to go heeled all the time."

"Okay. Now what happens to Wally? You recognized him. You're a cop. Are you taking him in? Like Sergeant Smith would? Or do you give him a break because you ain't a cop right now, only a father?"

Chad turned around in his chair so that he was looking straight at Wally, who was still lurking in the deepest shadows of the room.

"I've got a word of advice, speaking as Sergeant Smith.

Wally is going to be caught. If I don't get him, someone else will. He committed a crime and he'll have to pay for it."

"Like I always said, a fuzz is always a fuzz," someone shouted angrily.

"Be quiet," Chad spoke even louder. "But if Wally walks into my office tomorrow and gives himself up, that's going on his record and when I'm asked to help make up a probation report on him, that fact will be at the head of it."

"You're not taking him now?"

"As Papa Smith I don't have that authority."

Freddie looked around the room. "This guy's kid takes after him. He talks straight. Mr. Smith, do you know why Wally lifted those watches?"

"I don't know why and it doesn't make any difference to a cop. But as a civilian father, I'll listen."

"He got a chance to go for a job and he needed some clothes. His old man don't give him anything and his old lady don't care. Wally never been any place in his life but around here."

Chad glanced at his daughter. "I think that's the main subject of your theme. It's what you came to find out. If I'd pulled the trigger it would have been a horrible mistake."

"Yes, Dad," Cindy said.

Chad arose. "Good night, gentlemen," he said. "Thank you for allowing me to visit your club."

For one long, anxious moment nobody moved away from the table. The circle was as tight as ever. Then one man stepped back and the others followed.

"So long, Sergeant Smith," Freddie said.

"Good night," Chad responded. He looked straight at the figure hovering in the shadows. "Good night to you, Wally. I'd like to see you around—somewhere around my office. You've nothing to be afraid of."

When he took Cindy's arm, he could feel the tightness of her muscles. She was frightened, but not a trace of it showed on her face. One of the boys opened the door for them and they went out.

Chad unlocked the car with his set of keys, helped Cindy in, walked around the car and slipped behind the wheel. As he drove past the corner, he signaled the waiting radio car that everything was in order. The driver waved and pulled away from the curb.

"Do you think I was foolish to see those boys?" Cindy asked.

"Yes, don't you?"

"I was scared at first, but they were just kids like me. Misinformed about a lot of things and I guess they could become dangerous, but we got along fine."

"Until Freddie saw you riding with a cop."

"They were a little angry about that. I told them I didn't mention the fact that my father was a policeman because I was coming to them as one teenager to another, not as a cop's daughter, and it didn't make any difference who my father was."

"They bought it?" Chad asked in something close to awe.

"They asked more questions and they weren't going to give me any more information but I talked them into it."

"Do you think Wally will give himself up?"

"Yes. All he needed was someone to tell him what to do. To let him be himself. I felt sorry for him right away. Gosh, Dad, he's never been anywhere."

"I want your promise you won't do anything like this again, Cindy. Don't misunderstand me. Those kids weren't dangerous, but so many like them are. So very many."

"I give you my word. It was foolish. I admit it. Are you angry?"

He glanced at her with one of his slow smiles. "Of course not. I'm proud of you. Now I see a phone booth ahead. Please call your mother and tell her everything's fine."

Betty was still worried even after the phone call and she met them at the door. She quickly took Cindy in her arms and hugged her.

"Cindy was getting material for her theme," Chad said. "A little more first-hand than I approve of, but you can be proud of her."

"I'm proud of all my kids," Betty said.

"Mom, may I stay up later than usual so I can finish the theme while everything is hot in my memory?"

"Of course you may. Go on, get on with it."

Cindy fled to her room and in moments they could hear the pecking of her typewriter. Chad told Betty what had happened.

"She could have been in serious danger," he said. "Especially after she'd been discovered to be a cop's daughter. One thing she did accomplish—I now have the proof that I was right in not bringing down that boy. I'd have been sick now if I had. And that reminds me. I'm going to wake up Brian."

"He's not asleep. He's been muttering all night about not being allowed to go camping."

Chad opened the door to his son's room and walked in to sit down on the edge of the bed.

"You can go camping next Saturday," he said. "I changed my mind."

Brian sat up quickly. "No kidding, Dad?"

"No kidding. Tomorrow you and I will go out and buy some camping equipment. I'm going with you and your friends."

Brian's face fell. "Gosh, Dad. . . ."

"Do you want your father to be someone who never gets to go no place? Besides, you need someone to show you how to cook hot dogs and hamburgers or you'll starve to death. Is it okay?"

Brian sank back against the pillows. "Yeah . . . I guess so. But it won't be the same unless you buy me a sleeping bag for myself."

"You'll have one. Go to sleep. We'll talk about it tomorrow."

"Good night, Dad," Brian said. "I guess it'll be all right. You coming with us, I mean."

"Thank you, son. It will be my pleasure."

Chad closed the door softly and went downstairs to tell Betty all about it.